# Somewhere They Die

# Somewhere They Die

## L. P. Holmes

**Thorndike Press** • **Chivers Press**
**Thorndike, Maine** **Bath, England**

This Large Print edition is published by Thorndike Press, USA and by Chivers Press, England.

Published in 2000 in the U.S. by arrangement with Golden West Literary Agency.

Published in 2000 in the U.K. by arrangement with Golden West Literary Agency.

U.S. Hardcover  0-7862-2981-0 (Western Series Edition)
U.K. Hardcover  0-7540-4372-X (Chivers Large Print)
U.K. Softcover  0-7540-4373-8 (Camden Large Print)

The text of this Large Print edition is unabridged.
Other aspects of the book may vary from the original edition.

Set in 16 pt. Plantin by Al Chase.

Printed in the United States on permanent paper.

**British Library Cataloguing-in-Publication Data available**

**Library of Congress Cataloging-in-Publication Data**

Holmes, L.P. (Llewellyn Perry), 1895–
    Somewhere they die / by L. P. Holmes.
        p.    cm.
    ISBN 0-7862-2981-0 (lg. print : hc : alk. paper)
    1. Large type books.  I. Title.
PS3515.O4448 S68 2000
    813'.52—dc21                                    00-064793

# Somewhere They Die

# CHAPTER 1

On cresting the Chevron Mountains, the four-car combination freight and passenger train moved from rain's dismal grayness into the swirling drift of a late spring snow squall. Beyond the windows of the lone passenger coach the outer world resolved into a smother of white, and the pound of the engine's exhaust up ahead became a muted throb. Inside the coach, fading daylight dulled to gloom and the squall's chill struck swiftly through.

Stirred from a fitful doze by the biting reach of the cold, Riley Haslam lowered booted feet from the reversed seat in front of him, straightened up, and snugged his faded jumper a little more tightly across the solid bulk of his shoulders. The benefit of this was more illusory than real, and he murmured profane protest against the discomfort.

Low as he kept his voice, his words reached further than he intended, and he saw by the slight turn of the girl's head and the stiffening of her shoulders that she had heard. Just a little louder, he spoke again.

"Sorry. I wasn't thinking."

And by the faint tinge of color that brushed her cheek, he knew she had heard this, too.

She was in the second seat ahead of him and she had got on at White Falls Junction, where Haslam and Ben Spawn and the other three saddle hands had changed from the overland to this ancient branch-line rattler. Haslam had already stowed his sacked saddle, reversed the seat immediately in front of him, couched his feet on it, and settled back in what comfort he could find when she came down the aisle, carrying a small gripsack. Spawn and the others had taken seats up toward the forward end of the coach. The girl, after surveying the situation for a barely hesitant moment, had decided on her present spot.

They were the only passengers. Shortly out of White Falls the conductor, a scrawny individual with a tired-looking, tobacco-stained mustache, had come through, collected tickets, and then gone back to the crummy. One of Spawn's group had produced a deck of cards and the four of them started up a game of stud, using a pilfered seat cushion as a table. They had thrown an inviting look Haslam's way which had awakened not the slightest interest on his part, for he was a solitary sort by habit and choice and so he had retreated into a taciturn shell and slept and dozed by turns.

Now, up ahead, the laboring throb of the engine turned to a softer, easier cadence and the speed of the train picked up as it began coasting on the down-grade miles along the eastern flank of the mountains. It suggested the nearing end of a tiresome trip and Haslam, erect now in his seat, reached for tobacco and papers. The poker game, waging a losing fight against fading daylight, broke up. Ben Spawn got to his feet and came back along the aisle, legs spread wide and thick torso swaying to the lurch and swing of the coach.

Haslam thought Spawn was going to stop and speak to the girl. Evidently she did, too, for she turned her head with marked abruptness and stared out of the window beside her. The bite of a quick anger pulled at Spawn's face over this pointed rebuff. Then he shrugged, his lips took on a mocking curl, and he dropped into the seat beside Haslam.

"Miss Cora Wilkerson," said Spawn. "And proud, oh — very proud. Though I wouldn't know what about."

Haslam's reply was curt. "Her own affair entirely, I'd say."

Spawn stared at him narrowly and Haslam met the look with a cool reticence that gave not an inch before Spawn's arrogant and thrusting temper. Spawn's rough tone took on an added heaviness.

"I've seen them more sociable than you, Haslam."

Haslam, spinning his smoke into shape, lipped and lighted it before answering. "Wasn't hired to be."

Spawn jerked his head. "The boys yonder are beginning to wonder about you."

"If it amuses them, who cares?"

"Maybe," said Spawn, "I'm beginning to wonder a little, myself."

Haslam shrugged. "And I should be concerned about that?"

"You're damned right!" A flash of quick anger heated Spawn's eyes, and he settled hard-gripping fingers on Haslam's arm. "Listen, mister! When I hired you —"

Riley Haslam's free hand chopped down, driving Spawn's grip aside. "Friend, don't ever do that!" The words were low, but they carried a harsh ring. Again came the clash of glances and it was Spawn who looked away.

"Better!" said Haslam. "Now suppose we get something straight, Spawn. You hired me on to ride for somebody by the name of Overdeck. That I expect to do. But the deal said nothing about me sitting into a poker game when I prefer my own company. And there was nothing in it about letting you or anybody else push me around. If you don't like it that way, we'll call everything off, right now!"

"Like hell we will!" Dark blood flushed Spawn's heavy face. "Syl Overdeck's money bought you a railroad ticket to Palisade and fed you along the way. You'll work out the price of that — or —"

"Or — what?"

Spawn got to his feet, stared down at Haslam. His cheekbones were high and shelving, and they seemed to push his eyes into small, heated pits.

"You'll see, Haslam. You want to play the lone wolf, do it and be damned to you. But don't try going bucko on me. It just won't work!"

Spawn went back up the aisle. The conductor came in again and lit the lights of the coach. Their thin, yellow glow spread a doubtful radiance. Haslam hitched a shoulder point against the sill of his window and put his glance on the dusk-blurred run of country sliding by.

The train had moved out of the snow

squall into a land of steadily thickening timber, with black upthrusts of lava lifting darkly here and there. A low rim of that same black lava slid by, catching the rumbling echoes of the train's progress and throwing them back flat and broken. It was country which Haslam noted only subconsciously, for his thoughts had turned inward and now laid a strict soberness across his face.

He'd turned thirty on his last birthday. To his name he possessed the clothes he sat in, his sacked saddle and gun and other frugal gear, and some three or four dollars remaining of the fifteen which Ben Spawn had staked him to for eating money along the tiresome drag in from the Skull River country.

This job that lay ahead? He could guess pretty well what it would be like. Just like a dozen others he'd left along the back trail. For Ben Spawn hadn't fooled him a bit. In the first place there had been the approach. Out of nowhere, and a complete stranger, Ben Spawn had dropped in beside him at a bar and offered to buy a drink. And strangers just didn't accost another in that manner without some purpose. But because Haslam had ridden away from one job only lately and was wondering where the next one was coming from, he'd accepted the drink and listened to Spawn's offer.

Ben Spawn had said he was looking for saddle hands. Men to ride for one Syl Overdeck, on a range beyond the Chevron Mountains. Which was the second tip-off. Ranchers didn't go looking for saddle hands — regular saddle hands — several hundred miles away from a home range. They just didn't have to.

This fellow Spawn, Riley Haslam knew, was hiring something more than just average saddle-hand ability. What he was really hiring was the gun he'd seen on Haslam's hip, and the cold and reckless something which lay behind Haslam's eyes. There would be, Spawn had explained, a railroad ticket to Palisade, and eating money along the way. After that, Syl Overdeck would take over.

Riley Haslam had considered the offer for only a short time before nodding agreement. It really didn't matter, one way or another. Here was that next job he'd been wondering about, and it would be time enough after he reached Palisade to find out what it really called for.

A long jump into new country, with a gamble as to what lay at the end. It all fitted in with the restless, footloose way of life that

13

had eaten up the last twelve years of his existence. A man, it seemed, could drift into a certain groove of living when he was young enough to like the danger and movement and irresponsibility of it, then find suddenly that it would become fixed, like any other habit. And this, even after the flavor of it had begun to go bitter and flat on his tongue.

Turned thirty and still just a saddle bum with a potent gun and a certain something poised behind his eyes that gave other men pause. That, mused Riley Haslam bleakly, was what he added up to at this moment. And, any way you looked at it, it was a damned small amount.

Ben Spawn? Hell! He'd met up with plenty like Spawn. From some of these, because of the sheer need of holding a job and thus having a place to sleep and food to put in his belly, he'd taken the weight of authority. With others, he'd knocked the chip off their shoulders and faced them down with a cold ruthlessness that had, on one range, earned him the sobriquet of "Black" Riley Haslam. Which, he decided, was nothing to find any pride in, either.

His cigarette had gone out. He thumbed another match from his jumper pocket, dragged it across the sole of a boot. In the uncertain glow of the coach's lamps he looked through the pale drift of tobacco smoke at the trim outline of the girl's head. She had taken off her hat, and her hair, neatly parted and drawn back into a heavy knot at the nape of her neck, was chestnut brown, thick and fine. Her straight shoulders, trim under the folds of her coat, swayed with easy balance and grace to the lurch and swing of the coach, and it was Haslam's vague thought that she was probably no stranger to a saddle, knowing that kind of unconscious poise.

Beyond Haslam's window the world was now almost fully dark. Trapped by the timber pressing in on either side, the engine's breath of coal smoke and wet steam wreathed the train in coiling masses. The whistle tossed back its lonely cry in a long, wailing banner of sound, and shortly after this the clacking tempo of the wheels began to slow.

The scrawny conductor came in at the rear end of the coach, said "Palisade!" in a nasal drone, then went on through. Ben Spawn and his group of three got up and moved toward the forward platform of the car.

Haslam stood, arched his chest, stretched, then shouldered his sack of gear and moved into the aisle. The girl, who had donned her hat once more, was also on her feet. For a moment her glance met Haslam's fully, and he was startled when she spoke.

"You don't look like a fool. Yet you'll be one if you ride for Sylvanus Overdeck and do his dirty work. For he'll use you and see you killed and pass you by without another thought."

Riley Haslam decided that she was nice to look at. He tipped his head slightly.

"For your advice, thanks. About anybody killing me and passing me by, I could have something to say about that. Yet a job is a job and a man has to eat."

Her chin tilted a trifle. "That's what the man said who robbed a bank. He had to eat."

Just a hint of a smile pulled at Haslam's lips. "You make it sound pretty bad. What kind of country am I moving into, anyhow?"

She did not reply immediately, just stood studying him with an impersonal directness that tightened Haslam's smile. "Hard case," she decided finally, "with a few of the instincts of a gentleman."

Haslam's tone ran dry. "Thanks for that last remark. Sets me up. Saves my self-respect."

16

She flushed slightly, turned and went down along the aisle ahead of him. The train jolted and creaked to a halt, and up ahead the engine panted and wheezed like something old and tired. Ben Spawn and his group, crowding the coach steps, dropped off into a world where dusk had thickened to a chill darkness. Windows of a station house winked with light, and beyond, across a wide flat, a scatter of yellow glints proclaimed the town of Palisade.

Just ahead of him, Haslam watched the girl step down and he heard a clear, feminine voice call, "Over here, Cora!"

The girl answered, "All right, Babe."

Came a man's voice, hard and compelling, edged with triumph. "I got your wire from White Falls, Cora. Well, no time like now to take care of that little matter. Come on, boys!"

Riley Haslam, leaving the train, felt the crunch of cinders under his boot heels. Raw, cold air, rank with the breath of the train, struck his nostrils. Light, lancing thinly from the windows of the coach, made a yellow lane along which the girl moved toward three waiting figures.

Two of these were partially indistinct, at the outer edge of the lane of light. But the third loomed tall and broad, his head and shoulders caught in the light's fullest glow. Haslam got a fleeting impression of bold features in a full-fleshed but solid face, and of teeth gleaming white against deeply weathered skin in an exultant, confident grin.

These things Riley Haslam saw, while the words he'd just heard spoken were a half-formed echo in his mind, as was the significance of them. Then, as sharpening instinct began to take over, he stiffened to a taut and deepening awareness.

For there was the scuff of boot heels, the muted jangle of spurs, and the shadowy blur of figures moving in. Off to Haslam's right sounded the hard, spatting impact of a blow, followed by a pain-filled curse and then by Ben Spawn's rough, gravelly exclamation.

"What the hell —"

Somebody said, "Here's one of them!" And then a man's hard-charging bulk drove into Haslam.

A fist, slashing in out of nowhere, slammed against the side of Haslam's head, staggering him, sending an exploding burst of light rocketing crazily before his eyes. He dropped his sack of gear, then stumbled over it and went to his hands and knees as a second man lunged into him from the side.

Somebody dropped on him, winding an arm about his neck. A hard fist clubbed again and again his head. A boot drove into his ribs. A man exclaimed pantingly:

"Keep him down, Pres — keep him down! Keep him down and whip the fear of God into him!"

So far, sheer surprise and the stunning effect of that first smash to the head had left Riley Haslam unable to defend himself. But now he braced a left hand on the cinders, reached up and back with his right, found a head of shaggy hair under his clawing fingers, gripped hard and hauled over and down with a rolling twist of his shoulders.

The owner of the hair yelled his quick agony, came whirling off Haslam's back. Haslam reared half up, then came down with bunched knees driving into the fellow's body, smashing the breath from him. Haslam got his feet under him and came fully erect, a big man, filled now with a black and wicked anger.

He sensed another figure charging in on him, and he threw a blow that shut off a flow of angry curses and drove the attacker spinning. For the space of a brief breath or two, Haslam stood alone and in the clear, getting hold of the sound and action around him.

Over there, men were battling furiously, a

dark knot of figures, mauling and panting. Blows sounded suddenly and a man's high, thin cry of sudden agony echoed through the gloom.

Riley Haslam had no time to hear more, for they were at him again, three of them now. They closed with him, trying one moment to wrestle him down, then throwing wildly mauling fists at him the next. It settled into a mad, savage tangle, there in the raw darkness, where no holds were barred and anything went. Haslam fought them with a silent, cold fury, thinking longingly of the gun he'd stowed away in his sack of gear when he first took the train.

They whirled and lurched and crashed into the side of the train coach, then bounced off and battled away from it. A man got in close and lunged upward, driving his head into Haslam's mouth, and then Haslam tasted the salty hotness of his own blood and felt the drip of it begin to slime down his chin. He retaliated with a bunched knee ramming into the fellow's body, knocking him back. But Haslam's advantage was short, for a fist winged in again from the side, landing solidly on his temple, staggering him and leaving an aching numbness in its wake. The one who threw the punch lifted a warning yell.

"Over here, Hugh — over here! This one's a tough bastard!"

So now came another, storming at Riley Haslam, a man who was laughing gustily with the sheer savage joy and triumph of this thing. Haslam hooked a punch, felt it land, and the big man's laugh broke off abruptly. Yet he slid under Haslam's next try and then they were chest to chest, locked in blind, primitive conflict.

In Riley Haslam there lay the solid power of big bones and tough sinews. But this fellow who had hold of him was all he wanted to try and handle. For a short moment it was a dead even thing, this initial test of strength. Then there were others to aid Haslam's antagonist and they had the weight and numbers on him and the battle began going inevitably against him.

They drove him back, stubborn step by stubborn step. He took blows and he landed them. But he was one against several and he had to keep retreating or be completely overwhelmed. Abruptly the edge of the railroad station platform was against the back of his legs. He understood the danger of this and tried to fight his way clear. But there were too many of them and they bent him back and over until he went down, the rough, splintery planks of the platform grinding against his shoulders.

A hand found his throat, locked there, choking off his breath. A big fist beat into his face again and again. Haslam's senses began to rock and blur. Those crashing blows seemed to blind him, and twice a boot drove into his side, leaving a deep and tearing agony.

Now another yell sailed across the night. "Here's Spawn, Hugh! Here's Ben Spawn — and he's getting away —"

That clubbing fist ceased to batter Haslam and some of the weight went off him. A man's panting words fell harshly.

"Your tough bastard is softened up now, Steg. You and Pres can finish the job. Make it a good one!"

So now there were just two of them and for a moment Haslam lay limp, letting them have their brutal way with him, with their knees and fists and trampling boots. Then Haslam half rolled, crooked a knee and drove his boot savagely into a man's chest. After that there was only one.

This one would have yelled for help again, but Haslam, following that driving boot upward, got a clawing hand on the fellow's throat and choked back the cry. The foe, pulling back frantically in an effort to break free, hauled Haslam up with him. They swayed and stumbled across the platform and brought up with a crash against the wall of the station house. The impact seemed to spring open a door right beside them.

Light gushed out and in its glow stood a short, fat man in striped bib overalls, bald-headed and with wide, bulging eyes staring out of a round red face. Haslam threw his man straight into that frightened countenance, lurched on, fell off the far end of the platform and crawled on hands and knees into the black sanctuary of the darkness beyond.

For a little time he stayed so, hunched and sick. Then he got his hands against the end of the station house and with this support managed to push once more to his feet. He stood there, hands braced against the wall, his feet spread, his head sagging. Breath ran in and out of him in hoarse, shuddering gulps, with every inhalation hurting clear to the bottom of his lungs. Those kicks in the ribs — they must have broken something. . . .

The harsh taste of blood was on his lips and the muscles of his legs were crawling and shaking with weakness. But for the support of the station wall, then he must certainly have gone down again, there in the whirling dark. He was half blind and more thoroughly used up than ever before in his life. Yet there was that black fury burning and raging in him. If he only had his gun — his gun — ! What a fool he'd been for not wearing it instead of stowing it away in his sack of gear. . . .

Inside the station house sounded voices, one scared and shrill and yapping, the other hoarse and thick. Then this second voice was bawling through the night again.

"He got away from Pres and me, Hugh — he got away!"

The answer came back, roaring angry. "Find him, damn it — find him! Couldn't the two of you handle him? Get after him!"

Haslam blinked painfully as the import of this struck home. They weren't done with him. They'd start in on him again, once they found him. And he was about through; he had nothing left to fight with. They'd certainly find him if he stayed where he was, so he pushed away from the station wall and went stumbling and reeling across the open dark.

That town yonder, where the scattered lights glimmered, maybe somewhere over there he might find a dark corner or cranny into which he could crawl and lay hidden until he got back some of his strength. He was a stranger in a strange land, but still there must be some place. Maybe he might even be able to locate a gun. That was it! That was what he wanted — a gun! Then, damn them, he'd show them!

He heard them ferreting around the station house, calling back and forth. He tried to increase his pace. Twice he stumbled where there was nothing to stumble over, and the second time he went to his hands and knees. He was trying to get up when running steps came swiftly and lightly in on him.

He reared back on his haunches, snarling soundlessly like a crippled and cornered wolf. He had a clenched fist drawn back, ready to strike. But he never threw the blow, for the voice which reached him was soft and sympathetic and breathless.

"Please! I want to help you. You can't stop here or they'll find you, surely. Quick! Lean on me!"

Here was lithe strength to help him to his feet, and then the soft roundness of a shoulder to steady and aid him. Here also, as his head wobbled and bent in its weakness, were tendrils of windblown hair flicking across his beaten face, hair that gave off a faint, clean fragrance.

Somewhere in the night a man's deep

voice was calling, half in anger, half in anxiety.

"Janet — where the devil are you? Janet — you hear me?"

There was no answer, but at Riley Haslam's side that breathless voice was urging him to shambling movement.

"Quick! We must go on!"

Buildings loomed in front of them and they circled to the dark rear of these, Haslam's companion guiding his steps. Behind them further outcry lifted.

"Nobody around the station, Hugh. He must have cut for town!"

"Then get after him. Spread out and get after him!"

Now the rear of a big, square-shouldered two-story building loomed above them. Out in back of them men were running through the dark, calling to each other. Haslam moved heavily, blindly along, heeding as best he could the now almost frantic urgings of his benefactor.

Lord, how weak he was! Brutal the fight had been, but how could it have taken so much out of a man? Must have been those kicks that did it. Must have broken a rib or two, surely, from the pain that gnawed at him.

The slim figure at his side was murmuring

something, like a thought spoken aloud. "—
if only it's unlocked — only unlocked —"

She left him for a moment, then was
swiftly back, exclaiming with soft exultancy.

"It is unlocked. Now you'll be safe!"

With her guiding him, they turned in from
the night through a door that led into utter
blackness. She closed the door behind
them, then spoke a warning.

"Careful now, there are stairs ahead."

She was guiding him again, but even so
his shuffling feet struck the lower step and
he fell against the rest. The stairs creaked
and rattled, making what seemed to Haslam
an unholy racket. Up above a door opened,
letting out a flare of light. A woman's voice
struck down at them.

"Get out of there! No drunk sleeps off his
whiskey on my back stairs. Go on — get
out!"

"It's no drunk, Mother Orde," answered
the girl. "It's Janet Wilkerson — with a
man."

There was an exclamation of amazed
misbelief. "Janet Wilkerson! Child, what on
earth — A man you say? What man — and
why —"

The speaker now appeared in the lighted
doorway above, carrying a small lamp. A
gray-haired figure, she came down a step or

two, lifting the lamp high. "What man?" she asked again. "What's the matter with him?"

"He's been badly beaten," explained the girl. "Hugh Racklyn and some of his riders did it. They're still looking for him."

To bear out this statement came a yell in the night beyond the walls.

"Try again, damn it — try again! Hugh says to try every back door. Maybe the one to the Staghorn —"

"You see," said the girl. "Can I bring him up there, Mother Orde?"

"Of course — of course! Bring him up. That — that Hugh Racklyn!"

By aid of the light and the girl's supple strength, Haslam made the climb. The woman closed the door and pointed to a chair. Haslam sagged into it thankfully.

Now the lower outer door slammed open and there was the clatter of boot heels. A man cursed.

"Black as the inside of hell here. Scratch a match."

"And make a fat target should he throw a gun —"

"If he had a gun he'd have used it by this time. Scratch a match!"

The gray-haired woman cautioned Haslam and the girl with a finger on her lips. Then, after a short wait, she opened the upper door and sent a sharp demand downward.

"What's going on down there? Who is it?"

"Couple of Rocking R hands. We're looking for somebody."

"Looking for who? What on earth are you talking about, anyhow?"

"A man. A two-legged man. Did he come in here?"

"You don't see him, do you?"

"No-o. But maybe he climbed those stairs."

"And maybe he didn't! Who is this man you're looking for?"

"A gunfighter who came in on the train. Ben Spawn brought him in, so that means he figured to ride for Syl Overdeck. You mighty sure you ain't got him up there?"

"A stranger and a gunfighter?" The woman's voice mirrored a vast contempt. "Now I know you're crazy. Get along with you and quit making all this racket."

"All right," came the grudging reply. "But if you've taken him in, Hugh Racklyn will —"

"That's enough!" broke in the woman curtly. "Don't try and bully me with mention of Hugh Racklyn. He may be God to himself and certain gullible fools. But never to me. Now, get out!"

She closed the door, locked it and stood listening. From below came some thwarted mumblings, a growled curse or two. Then the outer door slammed. The woman moved over to a table and set her lamp down. She stood in front of Riley Haslam, hands on ample hips, studying him.

"So that's it, eh?" she said. "Another gunfighter brought in across the mountains to clutter up the clean earth." She turned on the girl, her tone severe. "Janet, do you know this man? Have you ever seen him before?"

"No," admitted the girl readily, "never before tonight. But does that make any difference? And somebody in the Wilkerson family had to do something to try and make up for Cora's silliness."

"Cora's silliness? I don't understand."

"It was Cora who sent word ahead to Hugh Racklyn that this man — and others were on the train. So Hugh and his men were waiting at the station. The moment this man stepped off the train — like the others — they were set upon and beaten. I — I don't care if he — they are gunfighters and set to ride for Syl Overdeck — it was low-down and cowardly on Hugh Racklyn's part. And he goes on making a fool of Cora — and Dad."

The gray-haired woman's tone softened. "You'll always be a completely sweet kid, Janet — chasing your generous impulses. I hope nobody will ever misunderstand them. Your dad gets the straight of this, he'll skin you alive."

"I'm not afraid of Dad," was the serene answer. "It's Hugh Racklyn who scares me. Not for myself, of course, but for Cora. Where that man's concerned, she can't see any further than the end of her good-looking, but sometimes awfully silly nose. And there are times when Dad is almost as bad."

The gray-haired woman turned back to put her measuring glance on Riley Haslam again.

"Now that we got him," she said tersely, "what are we going to do with him?" She shrugged as she added, "Following their impulses, women can get themselves into the damnedest tangles."

# CHAPTER II

Under the tide of returning strength and vitality, Riley Haslam had straightened in his chair. Now, between bruised, puffed lids, he met the gray-haired woman's glance and held it. He spoke past battered lips, his words a little thick and clumsy.

"Whatever the impulse, I'm grateful for it." His tone cleared up a trifle as a brittle harshness crept into his voice. "If you can tell me where I can locate a gun, I'll take myself off your hands."

He made as if to get to his feet, but she pushed him back with a quick hand. Her voice turned softer. "Now you're being foolish. You stay right there. Janet didn't drag you in out of the night and I didn't let her bring you up here just so you could turn right around and go get yourself in trouble again. What's your name?"

"Riley Haslam."

She studied him again, seeing a rangy figure of a man whose solid shoulders were beginning to straighten and square again.

Past his swollen lids his eyes were a cold, steady blue, and under his bruises his features were rugged and hard and deeply weathered. His hands, sagging loosely between his knees, were square and powerful. She smiled slightly.

"They marked you up some, but I imagine more than one of them knew you were around. Those blundering fools who were looking for you — were they right in this? You intend to ride for Syl Overdeck?"

"They could be right."

"Maybe this evening's treatment has changed your mind about that?"

The line of Haslam's jaw tightened and the chill in his eyes turned them dark. "I want to meet Mr. Hugh Racklyn in daylight, and when the game isn't all one-sided."

Again he started to rise from his chair, but this time it was a savage gust of inner pain that stopped him. He caught his breath and pressed a hand to his side. A fine beading of sweat glistened on his face. He felt a small shade of embarrassment at what he thought had been a show of weakness, and he tried to keep the pain from drawing his voice thin.

"Some of that crowd were pretty free and enthusiastic with their boots when they had me down."

The woman showed quick concern. "Then it won't do to guess at matters. Doc Jay was sitting in a game downstairs a little while ago. I'm going to see if he's still there."

While speaking, she was moving toward an inner door of the room, which, standing open, disclosed a hallway beyond. She spoke across her shoulder to the girl.

"There's a glass and my toddy bottle on the bureau in my bedroom, Janet. I think this man could stand a good drink."

The girl followed her out, and Haslam could hear the murmur of their voices along the hall. Shortly the girl came back, carrying a glass holding a stiff three fingers of whiskey.

"Get outside of this," she ordered. "It will do you good."

Haslam took the glass, but before drinking looked at this girl with a grave steadiness, then spoke the same way.

"Janet Wilkerson. A name I'm going to remember a long, long time. Why you've done all this for me, I don't know. You had your own reasons, I guess. All I can do in return is to say thanks, and mean it as I never meant anything before in my life."

Her eyes held his without wavering, while color stole across her cheeks and ripened their sun-browned smoothness. She wore a divided skirt of forest-green twill, a wool blouse, a short, snugly buttoned buckskin jacket and a silk muffler tucked around her throat. Her small boots were well scuffed from use.

The eyes holding Haslam's glance so steadily were a clear hazel and, while her face was too high and broad across the cheekbones for true beauty, there was about her a certain exuberant vitality and sturdiness that was a loveliness in itself. Her age, he guessed, would be somewhere in the very early twenties.

"Why," he asked, "did you do it? Why did you snag me out of that ruckus?"

She frowned in thoughtfulness, her lips pursing. She shook her head. "I don't know," she said slowly. "I really don't know. Thinking about it now I just haven't any sane answer. You were just a reeling, stumbling figure in the dark, a person I'd never seen before and will probably never see again. Doesn't add up to a lick of sense, does it?" She glanced at the glass in his hand. "You're supposed to drink that, you know."

Haslam nodded, lifted the glass and downed the liquor. When he lowered the glass she had moved over to the door leading to that back flight of stairs and was turning the key in the lock. She paused to look at him again.

"No," she repeated, "I don't know why I did it." Then her lips pulled into what was more elfin grin than it was a smile. "But I'm glad I did. Because I like to bedevil certain people. Now I'm getting along. Tell Mrs. Orde I've gone to make peace with a father who I know is about ready by this time to take a quirt to me."

Before Haslam could say another word she had slipped out the door and her steps were a soft descending echo on the stairs. Then the soft rap of a more distant door closing and, after that, silence.

The warmth of the whiskey had taken hold in Haslam, stealing all through him, loosening him up and stilling the quivering tautness that had locked his nerves and muscles. He sighed deeply and looked around.

He was sitting in a parlor of sorts. There were several chairs besides the one he occupied, and against the far wall was a couch, covered with a gay Indian blanket. There was a fairly large center table and a smaller one in a corner, both with lamps on them. There was a single window at one end of the room, screened with drawn and colorful curtains, while several pictures filled space along the walls. Two big, braided rag rugs took up most of the floor. Nothing was overdone, but the feminine hand was apparent everywhere, and the room was filled with a neat comfort.

Here also was quiet, with little outside sound reaching in. Though he listened intently, Haslam could pick up no further evidence of the hunters trying to ferret out the hunted. He sagged a little deeper into his chair, marveling at the luck and circumstance that had brought him to this spot. And breathing another word of thanks to that girl who had aided him. Janet Wilkerson.

But now sound did reach him, the deep resonance of a man's voice approaching. Wariness leaped up in Haslam and despite the pull of pain in his side he was on his feet when the gray-haired woman, Mrs. Orde, and two men came along the inner hall and into the room. One of the men was spare and soft-stepping, still-faced, dressed in the somber black and white habiliments of the professional gambler. The other was a giant of a man, ruddy of cheeks and with a great shock of red hair. It was he whose voice carried the rumble of far-off thunder, and it was booming now.

"Every time the cards are coming my way,

it seems some confounded human jackass has to get himself shot, or knifed, kicked by a horse, or otherwise busted up. Then I got to leave —" He broke off, staring fiercely at Riley Haslam from under shaggy brows. "What's your trouble? Aside from a pushed-around mug, you look healthy enough."

Mrs. Orde spoke. "Quit your bellowing, Jason. I told you I thought it might be some broken ribs." She turned to Haslam. "Where's Janet Wilkerson?"

"Gone," he answered quietly. "She said to tell you she'd gone to make peace with a very angry father."

Mrs. Orde sighed. "That fine, impulsive youngster! Well, she's right about one thing. Rufe Wilkerson will be mad enough."

Dr. Jason Jay, his complaint softened to a deep-chested growl, put his satchel on the center table and moved over to Haslam. "Get that jumper and shirt off. We'll have a look at those ribs."

Haslam said, "I don't know when you'll collect your fee, Doc. Right now I'm just about broke."

"Humph!" rumbled Doc Jay. "Who said anything about a fee? If everybody in these parts who owed me a fee was to pay up, I'd be able to retire. And then there wouldn't be any more fun in life. Let's get these duds off."

Like all the rest of him, Doc Jay's hands were huge, yet he was surprisingly deft and gentle. He helped Haslam doff jumper and shirt and then he went to kneading and prodding at Haslam's hard-muscled torso, especially on the left side where the dark and welted bruises stood out so strongly. He watched the changing play of expression on Haslam's face as he worked.

"Nothing broken," he decided presently. "But a couple of the asternal could be cracked. Damn men who'll kick another when he's down!"

He dug around in his satchel and came up with some kind of a soothing ointment which he smeared on the bruises. Then he applied several windings of a wide bandage, drawn very tight. Haslam found the pressure strangely comforting.

"You should be as sound as ever in a week or ten days," said Doc Jay. "Providing, of course, that you don't get worked over in another ruckus. At that, you were lucky. Word is that Racklyn's crowd left a dead man over by the railroad station. They beat his head in with a gun barrel, so Sam Basile says. I'm going over there as soon as I finish with you. Now Mamie, if you can scare up a basin of water and a couple of towels . . ."

A few minutes later, his face washed clean

of blood and grime, shirt and jumper donned once more, Riley Haslam walked stiffly around the room, steady and fairly whole again. Doc Jay watched for a moment, then gave rumbling advice.

"If you're really smart, friend, you'll lay low until tomorrow, then catch the train out of here. For there's nothing in these parts for men like you but a violent death and a shallow grave, no matter which side of the fence you ride on. There's little to choose between Syl Overdeck and Hugh Racklyn. They're both arrogant, rapacious fools who'll destroy a lot of others before they destroy themselves. If you need money for railroad fare, I'll stake you."

Haslam squared around, met the glance of this red-headed giant with the mighty voice and the gentle hands. Here, he thought, was a man he could respect and like. But he shook his head, his battered lips pulling to a crooked mirthless smile.

"A man like me owns little enough, Doc — except pride. Probably it's not even a very good brand of pride, but it's all I have. And if I ran now, then I wouldn't have anything left. Obliged for the advice and everything else. But I think I'll stick around for a while."

Doc Jay shrugged. "Figured that would

probably be your answer. Well, I've been working on the human carcass for quite some time, and I can draw you a true picture of it, right down to the last inch of stubborn hide. But I doubt I'll ever be able to understand the perverse workings of the human mind. I wouldn't have offered the advice if I hadn't thought I saw something more to you than to the average run. I hope I won't ever be called upon to pronounce you dead, but, considering this and that, it could so come about. Anyhow, good luck!"

Dr. Jason Jay picked up his satchel and went out, floor boards creaking under his massive weight. Riley Haslam, lips twisted wryly, turned to the others.

"Nothing if not direct, that fellow. Well, it seems I'm in everybody's debt. I've a couple of dollars in my jeans, but not nearly enough to pay for all his kindness. Maybe someday I'll be able to make it up to you. Now I'll take myself off your hands." He looked at the woman. "Special thanks to you, ma'am. And I'll go out the way I came in." He moved to the door leading to the back stairway.

For the first time the gambler spoke, his voice as quiet and as expressionless as his face.

"You go out now and you'll walk right

into the very thing you were trying to get away from. Racklyn has men watching this town from end to end. They're not making the noise they were, but they're there. Racklyn's a bulldog in things like that."

Haslam met the gambler's intent glance for a moment, then showed a return of his former harshness. "If I can scare up a gun somewhere, I'll take care of myself."

The gambler shrugged. "Maybe. But I still say you'd be smart to stay under cover until morning. By that time Racklyn's hunting fever will have cooled off a lot."

The woman spoke. "It would probably help if we became a little better acquainted. You say your name is Riley Haslam. This is Cash Fletcher. I'm Mamie Orde. Cash owns the Staghorn. I manage the hotel end of it."

The gambler offered his hand quite readily. It was slender and white, but there was a startling element of steel in the grip of it. And for the first time the stillness of the man's face broke. He showed a fleeting smile.

"I know what's on your mind, Haslam. You're asking yourself — why? Why should complete strangers like Mamie and myself know any concern for your safety? Well, for one thing, it happens that we possess our share of the better human instincts. Perhaps, in the opinion of some, a man like me is not supposed to know any of those better instincts. Yet I do. Also, there could be more practical reasons, all of them strictly honorable."

Fletcher's glance was steady, and Haslam, after holding it a moment, nodded. "You've convinced me. If you've an odd corner where I could hole up —"

"Plenty of room in my quarters," said Fletcher. "And, when did you eat last?"

"Back at White Falls Junction," Haslam told him. "Sort of a running grab and gulp."

"We'll take care of that, too. Mamie, you'll tell Scuffy?"

"I'll tend to it," she nodded.

Cash Fletcher led the way out of Mrs. Orde's quarters. At the far end of the inner hall, some half-dozen stairs led down to a balcony which ran across one end and along one side above a big barroom. The balcony was wide enough so that by keeping close to the wall a person could pass along it and not be seen by anyone in the room below.

Down there, men were talking and drinking, and tobacco smoke coiled and hovered. There was a strong vein of excitement in the talk, having to do with the savage fight that had been waged at the railroad station. Most of the talk was indistinguishable to Haslam as he moved with Cash Fletcher along the balcony, but parts of it carried up fairly clear. He heard the name of Hugh Racklyn spoken and also that of Ben Spawn. Then he caught just a part of a man's remark.

"— told me that it was that oldest Wilkerson girl who tipped Racklyn off by a telegram over the railroad wire from White Falls —"

There was a door at the far end of the balcony and as Cash Fletcher opened this he said, "Wait until I get a light going."

A match flickered and then a lamp which took on a stronger glow. Riley Haslam stepped into the room and closed the door behind him. Here were comfortable quarters again, but a man's room with no frills. Everything was neat and orderly, with a center table, several chairs and a couple of made-up bunks. Fletcher pointed to one of these.

"Yours for the night. Make yourself at home."

Haslam took a chair and watched in silence as Fletcher produced bottle and glasses from a corner cupboard. He poured deftly and handed a glass to Haslam, who spoke slowly.

44

"Maybe the kind of life I've led has knocked a lot of illusions out of me. So while I'm not denying those better human instincts you spoke of, friend, I can't help but wonder if there isn't considerable more of something to all this. Am I right?"

Cash Fletcher, measuring the liquor in his glass against the lamplight, showed his faint smile.

"As rain," he readily admitted. "Believe I suggested as much a few minutes ago. It happens that while I like Syl Overdeck little, I like Hugh Racklyn even less, and I'm human enough to enjoy seeing him discomfited. Then there is another angle which we may come to later, depending on developments. For the present, suppose we leave it that, like Doc Jay, I think I see something more to you than the usual run." He lifted his glass. "Here's luck!"

Haslam drank, put his glass on the table, wiped his lips with the back of his hand.

"So there was a man killed tonight, out at the station," he murmured. "Just another drifting saddle hand with a gun, who got his head beat in because he was going to ride for the other side." His glance lifted. "This fellow Racklyn believes in playing it rough, doesn't he?"

"Decidedly!" Fletcher nodded with emphasis. "But Syl Overdeck is no better. You're stepping into something, Haslam."

"What's the big argument between the two?"

"Range — mainly. The Silver Glades country over past the Hatchet Rim. More definitely, perhaps, the point of access to that range from this side. Which would be Big Saddle Pass."

Cash Fletcher felt the impact of Haslam's steady glance and made a guess at the thought behind it. "You're wondering, maybe, at a professional gambler passing judgment on the shortcomings of other men?"

Haslam shook his head. "Not necessarily." Then he added, somewhat enigmatically, "Any man without some kind of an opinion of his own is a fool."

Beyond the door came the sound of approach along the balcony. The steps were uneven, shuffling. Fletcher opened the door.

The man who stood there, carrying a covered tray, was undersized, shriveled and warped. One leg seemed shorter than the other and swung awkwardly at the hip. His left shoulder sagged, producing a hunched, stooped effect. His scanty hair was white, his face seamed and puckered with deep lines. Faded eyes peered out, mild and apologetic.

Cash Fletcher took the tray. "Thanks, Scuffy," he said gently.

The little man nodded wordlessly, turned and shuffled away. Fletcher hooked a toe on the door, swung it closed, then brought the tray over to the table. A chill note rang in his voice.

"You just looked at Scuffy Elrod. Once he was a whole man, owning a cabin, a herd of at least two hundred and fifty head of white faces, plus the range known as the Deer Creek Meadows. Owning these meadows meant that he also controlled the western approach to Big Saddle Pass."

Fletcher paused while he moved the dishes from the tray to the table. Then he went on.

"One day Scuffy Elrod was found lying out in one of the meadows, all broken up and apparently dead. But he wasn't. And in a touch-and-go fight, Doc Jay brought him through, though Scuffy will never be anything like a whole man again. You saw how he's pulled to pieces physically. Mentally he does pretty good, though he's a little fuzzy there, too. And he's a mute. He lost his voice. He can't talk."

"Rough go," said Haslam soberly. "What had happened to him?"

A hint of dryness made Fletcher's tone

seem clipped. "Dragged by his horse, apparently. At least that seemed a part of the picture. The rest is guesswork."

"What's the rest?"

Fletcher shrugged. "Maybe someday I'll tell you. Right now, here's your supper. I'll have a cup of coffee with you."

Haslam ate hungrily, and the warm food and hot coffee brought him all the way back from his own beating. His face was stiff and sore with bruises and his bandaged ribs were a constant reminder. But these things were not of too much account, now that the full tide of strength and vigor had returned. Cash Fletcher produced cigars, and Haslam leaned back and savored the good weed in full content. He smiled slightly.

"A man's luck can be a strange thing. Not an hour ago I was hunting cover like a whipped animal. Now I sit here like this. I'm still trying to figure it."

Beyond the door steps again sounded on the balcony. Cash Fletcher's head lifted alertly and, when knuckles knocked, he called:

"Who is it?"

"Sam Basile."

Fletcher relaxed. "Come on in, Sam." Then, to Haslam, he added softly, "Town marshal."

The man who stepped in was stocky, dark-faced, a smooth, round swarthiness with black eyes that told nothing. He closed the door and stood with his back to it. He looked at Haslam and said, "Doc Jay told me about you."

Cash Fletcher nodded. "Meet Riley Haslam, Sam. What's on your mind?"

Sam Basile swung his pudgy shoulders with a small show of irritation.

"Couple of things. Mainly sore at myself for not getting over to the station in time to stop that ruckus. When I got there the worst was done with and Racklyn and his Rocking R gang had scattered. I did run into Steg Medill and I got him locked up. I'd like to charge somebody in that Rocking R outfit with murder."

Fletcher spoke slowly. "Unless it was Hugh Racklyn and you were able to make the charge stick, which I doubt, you'd be wasting your time."

"I know. But Medill can cool his heels overnight." Basile looked at Riley Haslam again, then reached in his coat pocket and produced a gun, which he laid on the table. "Yours?"

Haslam glanced at the weapon, nodded. "Mine."

"Had a hunch," said Basile. "There was a

sack of gear over by the tracks. The gun was in it, along with a saddle and some other stuff. The saddle had the initials R.H. stamped on the cantle. I lugged it all over to my office."

"Obliged," Haslam said. "What about the gun?"

"Depends. You a professional with it?"

"No. I can take care of myself pretty well, but I prefer to earn my wages like any other saddle hand, working cattle. At the same time I'm not too strong on this idea of turning the other cheek. I tried it a couple of times and got it damn well clouted."

"Generally works that way," was Basile's dry agreement. "You can keep the gun. You're a stranger here, but you've broken no laws that I know of. And any man has the right to protect himself. Doc Jay told me he tried to give you some advice. I'm saying it was good advice."

"Maybe," said Riley Haslam softly, a small, chill gleam flickering briefly and far back in his eyes. "But I'm stubborn about some things. Paying my debts is one of them. All kinds of debts."

The marshal sighed. "I'm stubborn, too. While you're inside the limits of my town, keep that gun in the leather. Else you'll look just the same to me as the next."

The ghost of a mirthless smile brushed Haslam's face. "Agreed."

"What was the name of the one who got hit too hard, Sam?" asked Cash Fletcher.

"Don't know. Have to get hold of Ben Spawn to find that out, I guess. Understand Spawn had hired him and was bringing him in. But Spawn ain't to be found just now."

"Maybe I can help you there," said Haslam. "Spawn introduced me to the other three in a sort of offhand way. What did this dead one look like?"

"Chunky built. Nose busted at some time and healed crooked. Towheaded, plenty. Almost like cotton."

"That would be Whitey Bryant, as I recall the name," Haslam said. "The other two — what about them?"

"Still runnin', I guess. Smarter than you." The marshal hitched his shoulders again in that irritated way and put his glance on Fletcher. "You know, Cash, there's one angle in this affair that rubs me plenty! The talk going around is that Cora Wilkerson sent a telegram in over the railroad wire to Hugh Racklyn, telling him that Spawn was bringing in him —" he nodded at Haslam — "and the other three. That don't set good with me at all. That's no play for a girl like her to make. She might have known what

Racklyn would do about it."

Fletcher took his cigar from his lips, stared at it for a moment of thought. Then he spoke gravely.

"Not necessarily, Sam. And when a girl like Cora is fond of a man, it's only natural she'd do what she figured would help him. And she's following along with her father's feelings in the affair, too. Fundamentally, there's nothing wrong with either Rufe or Cora Wilkerson. It's just that neither of them have yet opened their eyes to Hugh Racklyn's real makeup. Janet Wilkerson is the shrewd little monkey there."

"Ain't nothin' you can predict less than a woman," observed Sam Basile acidly. He turned to the door, then paused, looking back at Haslam.

"Where are you going to be, tonight?"

"Right here," Haslam told him. "Come tomorrow morning, I'll be my own man again."

"If you really meant that, you'd be smart," said Basile. "But I see you as Overdeck's man, and that's different."

Basile went out. Cash Fletcher began gathering up the dishes and stacking them on the tray.

"Sam's a pretty good man, but there's a limit to his worth. His intentions are good, but he talks a better grade of toughness than he owns. Now I got to get along. Some of the boys will be in tonight, wanting a game. Anything else you want?"

"Just a session with that bunk yonder," Haslam answered.

Fletcher nodded. "Nothing holding you back."

Alone, Riley Haslam relaxed with his cigar and let his thoughts run. Had he, a few hours ago, set out to figure what his reception in this town of Palisade would be like, the answer would not have remotely approached reality. Of one thing though, he'd had full proof; the viciousness of the attack by this Hugh Racklyn and his Rocking R crew had furnished that. This was a rough business he'd ridden into.

The chill crept back into his eyes as he pondered matters. The brawl had left a man dead, his head beaten in. That man could very well have been himself. Rough business, indeed!

Warm food and relaxation began to have their way and Haslam found himself yawning. The move awakened a twinge in his bandaged side, so he got up carefully, turned the lamp low and went over to his bunk. He grunted some and swore mildly at his stiffened difficulty in getting ready to turn in, pausing several times to let the sting of misery in his side abate. But presently he was in the blankets and at ease.

This building which housed the Staghorn was soundly built, but night's chill was beginning to strike through and the warmth of the blankets was a comfort. What sound there was, was merely a droning murmur, lifting from the bar and gambling hall. Cash Fletcher, it seemed, ran an orderly place.

Riley Haslam tried again to put his thoughts on the strange pattern of his fortunes, but all he managed out of it was the memory of a girl's soft nearness, guiding and urging him through the night to a place of safety, and then the picture of her as he'd last seen her, slipping through a doorway, showing him an elfin smile across her shoulder.

It was, he thought drowsily, the best memory to go to sleep on that he knew, and so that was the way it was.

It was nearing midnight when Cash Fletcher quietly entered the room. With him was Dr. Jason Jay. Fletcher turned up the lamp slightly and Doc Jay moved over and looked down at the sleeping Haslam, noting the sweep of jaw which, even in the relaxation of sleep, carried a certain grimness. Doc turned back, his booming voice throttled to a rumbling murmur.

"No, he's not the usual run, Cash. A tough one, no doubt. But it reaches further with him than just a fast gun and a bellyful of whiskey. There's a strong stamp of character here. This could be the man we've been looking for, all right."

Cash Fletcher showed his faint shrug. "We'll see. If Syl Overdeck makes a coyote out of him, then your character guess will be all wrong."

Doc moved to the door. "I'll stand on my judgment. I'd like to be on hand the first time Overdeck turns that damned nasty snarl of his on Riley Haslam. I'll bet the results will be interesting. Good night, Cash."

# CHAPTER III

At the far end of the balcony from Cash Fletcher's quarters, a stairway led down to the main floor of the Staghorn barroom, and just short of the entrance to the dining room. With twelve solid hours of healing sleep under his belt, Riley Haslam descended these stairs, moving a trifle stiffly. Cash Fletcher accompanied him. Hunger was a live and leaping thing in Haslam, sharpened by the aroma of fresh coffee drifting upward.

From the bottom of the stairs he had his full look at the bar and gambling hall. A swamper was at work, sweeping out, and chairs and poker tables made a sharp clatter in the morning's stillness as he pushed them here and there. A bartender was already on duty, serving a lone patron. The latter was a thin-faced, nondescript rider, who threw one quick glance at Haslam and Fletcher, then put his full attention on the glass of liquor in front of him.

Fletcher smiled faintly. "By name — Clip Parsons. One of the Rocking R crowd.

56

Hugh Racklyn's been wondering and guessing about you, Haslam. Now he'll know."

"And knowing, probably hold it against you for harboring me," Haslam said. "I'm sorry about that."

Fletcher shrugged. "You needn't be. Hugh Racklyn holds many things against me. I refuse to worry."

The Rocking R rider waited only for them to turn into the dining room. Then he downed his liquor at a gulp and hurried out.

Haslam paid strict attention to his breakfast until the first edge of hunger had been blunted. Then he sat back and fixed Cash Fletcher with a direct glance.

"Last night, when I remarked your kindness to me, you mentioned an angle. You didn't go into it any deeper then, so would you care to discuss it now?"

Cash Fletcher played with his thoughts for a moment, then his head came up and he met Haslam's regard with a long steadiness. In this moment these two men measured each other fully, Haslam almost grimly impassive, Cash Fletcher armored with his gambler's stillness of face and cloak of imperturbability. And each knew respect for the other.

"You came here to ride for Syl

Overdeck," said Fletcher. "You intend to go through with that?"

Riley Haslam nodded. "The man paid my railroad fare here and staked me to eating money. He did that on the promise that I'd ride for him. So I owe it to him to at least look his proposition over. As far as I know, I've never left an unpaid debt behind me yet — of any kind."

"Could be more to that remark than appears on the surface," observed Fletcher dryly. Then he added, "Syl Overdeck will collect anything you owe him, right down to the last thin dime. That's a card you can bet on. So, for the time, we'll let my angle ride."

"Right now," said Haslam, "I'm in your debt, too."

Fletcher shook his head. "Not at all. Isn't there an old saying to the effect that payment for some of the things we do is found in the doing? Something like that. Well, call this one of those things."

Again Riley Haslam measured this neat, inscrutable, still-faced man across from him. "You've done something to me," he admitted slowly. "You've everlastingly changed my opinion of gamblers."

Fletcher's almost austere front broke up in a quiet chuckle. "Better reserve judgment, Haslam, lest you be disillusioned.

Just the same, there are times when our blood runs as red as that of any other man. Well, what's your next move?"

"Collect my sack of gear from that town marshal of yours and then find my way out to Overdeck's headquarters."

"There's a plain trail to the place," said Fletcher. "Cuts to the left off the main road just south of town." Fletcher drained the last of his coffee, got to his feet and held out his hand. "Good luck!"

Over the handshake, Haslam said, "Thanks. I'll probably need it."

He built a cigarette, went out through the barroom to the street, and had his first daytime look at the town of Palisade. It was set down in the midst of a stretch of flat-running timberland. There was a single street, stretched in a partial curve, loosely fronted with buildings on either side. Some of these were of sawn lumber, others of peeled logs. West of town, toward the far side of a fairly extensive meadow, stood the railroad station, with a wye for turning and some cattle pens beyond. The rails of the main track, reflecting glints of morning's sunshine, swept north into the timber.

This same timber, touched by the sun, shone moist and gleaming, giving off its resinous fragrance. Wood smoke, drifting from

59

chimneys and coiling through the timber tops, added its own acrid tang, pleasant to the nostrils.

Moving slowly along the street, taking in the settled quiet of the place, Riley Haslam found it hard to believe that last evening this town had seen riotous violence in which one man had died. Yet the sore stiffness of his side and the ominous knowledge about the unfortunate Whitey Bryant were stern reminders of reality.

From a doorway just a little ahead of Haslam, two men stepped. One was Sam Basile, the town marshal. The other was a burly saddle hand with a face marked with cuts and bruises. There was a surly truculence about the fellow as he listened to what Sam Basile was saying.

"If I had any way of proving that you swung the gun barrel that killed that man, Medill — I'd hold you for murder. As it is, you can take this final word to Hugh Racklyn. Beyond the limits of this town I've no authority over what he and his outfit does. But if he brings any more trouble inside of Palisade, then I hold him personally responsible and I'm going after him the hard way. Savvy?"

Steg Medill shrugged, his manner contemptuous. "You try it and it'll sure as hell

60

turn out the hard way for you, Basile. You know that Hugh does what he damn pleases, and where. You know that as well as I do, so your big talk don't mean a thing. Now, how about my gun?"

Sam Basile made an angry gesture, but he pulled a weapon from his coat pocket and handed it to Medill, who checked it briefly before dropping it into the empty holster at his side. Then he squared around on Basile, defiantly ugly.

"You got the jump on me last night, else you'd never have got my gun in the first place. But you knew better than to try and keep it, didn't you? Well, know something else, Basile. From now on, jump or no jump, don't ever try and lift my gun again. For you just ain't tall enough to make it stick!"

Steg Medill emphasized the final words with a stabbing forefinger against Sam Basile's chest.

Riley Haslam had come up quietly on the pair of them. As he watched and listened, a cold fire began to burn in his eyes and bleakness thinned his lips. Medill — Steg Medill! Recalling the names he'd heard last night, Haslam knew that right here in front of him was one of the crowd that had mauled him personally, one who had done his dirty best to kick some ribs in. Yeah — Steg Medill!

Haslam missed none of the defiance Medill was throwing at Sam Basile. He saw the anger which crimsoned Basile's round, dark face. But he saw also that this anger had its distinct limits. It would never be cold enough or big enough to cause Basile to step past a certain line of caution. Sam Basile was going to take this insolence and defiance from Medill and do nothing about it.

What was it Cash Fletcher had said about this marshal last night? That Basile talked a better brand of toughness than he owned? Something like that, and plainly true. For it stood out strongly, now. Sam Basile might be long on intention, but he'd always be short on doing.

Before leaving Cash Fletcher's room that morning, Haslam had tucked his gun inside the waistband of his jeans and buttoned the lower half of his old jumper high enough to cover the butt of the weapon. Now he freed these buttons, leaving the jumper open and the gun clear to his hand. He moved swiftly in on the two men in front of him and his voice hit out, harsh and compelling.

"Get aside, Basile! I'll take him off your hands!"

They came around, the pair of them,

quick and startled. And at this moment, from the door of the general store across the street, Dr. Jason Jay and the store owner, Len Pechard, stepped into view.

Riley Haslam laid his fullest concentration on this Steg Medill fellow. Two strides from Medill and Sam Basile, he stopped.

"Yeah," he said again. "I'm taking him off your hands, Basile!"

Last night Sam Basile had seen Haslam in Cash Fletcher's quarters. And there he'd seen a man with a face hooded with bruises and sitting hunched over the misery of punished ribs. He had no idea then how tall Haslam stood, nor how wide across the back. He got the idea now. He made a verbal sop to his authority, but there was the stammer of defeat in it.

"No trouble, Haslam — I'll have no trouble! Last night you said you'd cause me no trouble. Now —"

"No trouble for you here, Basile," Haslam cut in. "But a pleasure for me — a big one! As for what I said last night, part of it was that I paid my debts — all of them. Remember? I should have added that on some things I collect, too. Like now! So you just step aside and let me handle things." While speaking, he did not look at Basile, all the pressure of his swelling anger reaching at Medill. Now, abruptly, his words were a raking lash. "All right, you! You got your gun back. What do you pack it for, balance?"

Steg Medill eyed Haslam with startled uncertainty, while trying to hold on to his show of bravado.

"Who is he, Basile? And what's rawhidin' him?"

"You know damned well who I am," charged Haslam bleakly. "Last night you and some of your crowd did your rotten best to kick my ribs in, or maybe cave my skull with a gun barrel like you did to that other poor devil. Me? Well, I'm the one you called the tough bastard. Remember? So, now we'll see. You just made a brag. About not having your gun taken away from you. Well, I'm going to take it, Medill. I'm going to take it and bat your ears off with it. That'll show you how a tough bastard plays, mister!"

Over in front of the store, Doc Jay and Len Pechard were held with a still and marked attention. They had no idea where this thing might lead, but they knew that at this stage there was nothing they could do about it.

As for Steg Medill, he was trying to meet Riley Haslam's boring stare and hold it. He wasn't up to the test. His eyes flickered and he backed up a step.

Sam Basile made another protest, but it died weakly in his throat at Haslam's curt order.

"Stay out of it, Basile!"

Steg Medill backed up another step. In his way he was a rough one. He owned a certain amount of brute courage. But he ran better with a pack than he did alone, with someone else to do the thinking and give the orders. He had already guessed Sam Basile's size and knew his limits. But he couldn't read this man now facing him, and just now he wasn't running with the pack. So he gave grudging way.

Haslam followed him, step by step. He watched the shine of desperation deepen in Medill's eyes, marked the start of sweat beginning to slime his face.

"What's the matter, Medill?" he taunted. "No spine when your man isn't down and without two or three others to help you?"

"Keep off!" blurted Medill thickly. "Don't push me too far!"

Haslam laughed frostily and with no mirth. "Going to push you plumb off the edge, Medill. Try and stop me!"

Steg Medill wanted to. He wanted to so badly the thick cords of his throat stood out and congestion behind his eyes put a wild, crimson flare in them. Yes, he wanted to but he couldn't. He just couldn't muster that last ounce of decision necessary to make him go for his gun and stake everything on the move. He took another step backward and then could retreat no further, for Haslam had been herding him toward the building and now Medill's shoulders were against the wall.

Then Riley Haslam closed in as he said he would — all the way. His right arm stabbed out, the palm of his hand flat, fingers spread. That open, spread-fingered hand slammed into Medill's face, framing it, driving Medill's head back against the wall with a sodden thump. Then Haslam's left hand reached out and down, grabbing at Medill's gun.

Now Medill made his break. He clawed for his gun with his right hand and with his left tried to jerk Haslam's forcing palm away. He failed in both, for Haslam's right arm was stiffly rigid and he was leaning his full weight behind it, half blinding and stifling his man. And Medill's frantically searching gun hand found Haslam's left fist in the way, as it dragged the gun free.

Riley Haslam stepped swiftly back, pulling his right hand from Medill's face. Then, as the bundled tension in Medill drove him lunging forward, Haslam brought his left hand, with Medill's gun gripped tightly, up and across in a short, savage slash. Flesh and bone and gun metal met with a muffled crunch.

Steg Medill's knees buckled and he started to slide down. Haslam hit him again, whipping the gun backhand from the other side. Medill's head rolled under the impact and he folded the rest of the way and lay in a heap at the foot of the wall. For a long moment Haslam stared at the man he'd whipped down. Then he turned to Sam Basile, holding out the gun.

"Give that to him when he gets his senses back. And tell him to keep out of my way from now on!"

Somebody was coming across the street. It was Doc Jay and his big voice was rumbling out ahead of him.

"Did you have to hit him the second time, Haslam? That was a little on the raw side, and unnecessary. I was prepared to like you. Now — I don't know!"

Haslam came around. "You don't know — what, Doc?" he asked softly.

They faced each other, two big men, their glances locked. Doc's shock of red hair was all abristle and those big hands, so deft and gentle at the art of healing, now clenched into big hard knots. Then he brushed past Haslam, dropped on one knee beside Steg Medill, straightening him out, swiftly gauging his condition. All the time Doc's anger was rolling in his throat.

"We'll say he had the first lick coming — but the second one could have killed him, and was completely unnecessary. For he was already unconscious, and falling!"

Riley Haslam had turned, was watching. Now he spoke with somber quietness.

"Last night, when you were working on my ribs, Doc, you said something. You said, 'Damn a man who'd kick in the ribs of another when he's down!' Yeah, you said that, Doc. Well, Medill was one of the crowd who did their best to kick mine in. The ribs are hurting now, to remind me. And maybe you're forgetting last night's dead one, Doc. The one with his head beat in. Well, the rules of that kind of game work both ways! Nasty facts, maybe — but true."

Haslam stepped past Sam Basile and went into the marshal's office. The sack of gear he was looking for lay in a corner and he shouldered this, then went out and angled up the street where, at the far end of the curve, a log-built stable stood, with a sprawl of corrals out back.

Doc Jay, his swift survey satisfying him

that Steg Medill would be all right, though he would carry scars, had straightened up. He stared after Haslam, the anger fading slowly from his face, being replaced by a troubled regret. His big voice softened to a modified rumble.

"Sometimes, when I get mad, I say things I don't entirely mean, Haslam. I did — just now."

Riley Haslam neither answered nor looked back.

Doc sighed deeply and looked at Sam Basile. "Let's get this one inside. I'll have to work on him."

Between them, they carried Steg Medill into Basile's office.

At the stable there was a roustabout who was anything but friendly. He looked Riley Haslam up and down with a surly eye before answering Haslam's question.

"We don't rent horses to strangers. Got a couple for sale if you're interested that way. But no rent business. For all I know, I let you have one, you might keep right on travelin'. Then we'd be out a bronc."

The chill that had begun to slowly fade from Haslam's eyes now flared up a trifle.

"Would you be trying to call me something in a lefthanded way? A horse thief, maybe?"

The stable hand held his ground. "I ain't tryin' to call anybody anything. I'm just givin' you the stable rules."

"I want a horse to ride as far as Syl Overdeck's layout," said Haslam. "The animal will be returned."

Haslam got another careful looking over. "You're hirin' on with Overdeck?"

"That's the picture."

The stable hand considered for a moment, then shrugged. "There's a Two Link bronc out in the corral. Ben Spawn left it there near three weeks ago and ain't been back for it. It's eatin' its head off and doin' nobody any good. You want to take that one and argue it out with Spawn later, I guess it'll be all right."

The horse was a line-backed dun and Haslam, when he had the animal saddled, turned to the stable hand again. "The trail to Two Link cuts off just south of town, doesn't it?"

"That's right. Main road runs due south into the Ash Pan Flat country. You turn east at the first break."

Haslam set his teeth against the pull of his sore ribs as he swung into the saddle, and he had a bad moment or two as the dun, full of ginger after long inactivity, showed an inclination to turn a little kinky. But he kept the animal's head up and by the time he was out in the street and moving along it, the dun was pretty well settled down.

The street lay empty under the warming touch of the morning's climbing sun. No one was in sight over in front of Sam Basile's office, where he'd left Steg Medill crumpled and senseless. Recalling Doc Jay's manner and words, the somberness in Haslam's face deepened. These, he had to admit, had jolted him. And now he asked himself why they should have, why he should give a damn, one way or the other?

In the past, the only opinion that had ever counted had been his own. For if a man gave too much concern to what others thought, then he could end up with no purpose of his own at all. Along a certain stretch of range, people might curse a man or they might bless him, yet when he rode away from that piece of country, it became just another part of a back trail that would never be retraced, and it all faded into forgetfulness and a spread of time of no consequence.

That was the way it had always been before. Of course, maybe it was the heedless uncaring of youth that had made it that way. Maybe, when a man grew older, he saw things in a little different light. Maybe he

71

began to unconsciously yearn for something more solid in life, and a big part of that solidity could be the good opinion of the kind of people who counted. Haslam shook his head, vaguely uncomfortable with the yeasting of such thoughts.

At the door of a saloon, the dingy front of which hardly lived up to its flamboyant title of "The Palace," a swamper showed, to squint at the sun, yawn, and then swing a languid broom. Past the Staghorn, the southern end of the street ran out into a stage station, a freighting yard and warehouse, and then a road cutting straight south and fairly well traveled by the signs.

The turnoff Haslam was looking for showed clear and he swung the dun into it. Within fifty yards he was out of sight and sound of town, for here ran unbroken, close-massed files of timber on either hand, which warded off the reach of the climbing sun and held imprisoned air which was still raw with last night's chill.

Riley Haslam rode with considerable wariness. He was remembering the rider who had been at the Staghorn bar when he and Cash Fletcher came down for breakfast, the one Fletcher had named as one of Hugh Racklyn's Rocking R hands. Past that, he was remembering last night, and he was too old a one at this rough business to be caught a second time.

Maybe, he thought grimly, he was considering himself in too important a role, but it didn't cost any more to be careful. And, apparently, this was that kind of country. A man rode with eyes and ears open, watchful of both sides and of his back trail as well, or he could end up dead.

Something like that was inferred by Doc Jay last night, after bandaging the sore ribs. Doc had said he hoped he'd never be called upon to pronounce him dead, but the inference was there that Doc figured he very well might be. And Doc was in a position to know about such things, for that was his job. Patching up those still worth patching, or giving the final word on someone for whom the trail had run completely out.

The dun was a good horse. Once settled down, it proved itself as a trail mount, moving with an easy-swinging, fast walk, barely short of a reaching jog, a pace which never broke and which ate up distance at a startling rate.

In time, the close-packed ranks of timber began to thin and here spikes of sunshine could break through and a man's vision reach out. Here too, cones of broken and jumbled lava jutted blackly up across the forest floor. Also, among the thinning conifers, thickets of scrub mountain oak and maple showed, new buds breaking into the softest shadings of pink and new, fresh green. The world smelled of hastening spring and its fine, strong vigor.

The trail cut past a jutting lava point that was tufted with silver-barked aspen, then dipped to a flat where willow clumps crowded beside the rushing waters of a fair-sized stream. Looking the ford over, Riley Haslam saw that the dun was going to get its belly wet. The horse went in cautiously, feeling its way, and Haslam had to bunch his knees to keep his boots dry. The water was crystal clear and icy cold, as Haslam found out when the dun, moving into shallowing water near the far side, churned up a spray that reached high enough to touch Haslam's face.

On this far side the trail, after cutting through some willows, moved into a type of country new in Riley Haslam's experience. Here was a broken, jumbled land of low lava ledges and cones, of potholes and flats, of scrub manzanita and matted thickets of mountain mahogany. Here were open sheets of barren lava rock on which the dun's hoofs ran hollowly, giving a man the feeling that he might be riding across the roof of some long-dead inferno. North and south it ran for miles, with an occasional gaunt pine or fir jutting up, lonely and subdued.

Straight east, some several miles away, a massive black lava rim towered, in some places its face almost sheer, in others steeply sloped, with slides of broken lava fragments. Across these slides thin thickets of chokecherry and mahogany crept timidly, and along the rim's crest, conifer timber again spiked the sky. North and south the rim marched, solid and unbroken to the south until it lost itself in mountains dimmed with distance. To the north it sagged, as though into a pass of some sort, before shouldering up solid and dark once more.

The impact of it caused Haslam to rein in and have his long and retentive look. He wondered if he'd ever seen a more savage and relentless-looking stretch of the world. Sometime, in dim ages past, the cataclysmic forces of a forming universe had been at work here, and the residue it had left still retained some atmosphere of the incredible fury that had mothered it.

If, mused Haslam, this country had spawned feud and gunplay and violent death, it was small wonder. For no man could call this kind of country home without taking on some part of its dark and bitter harshness.

He brought out his smoking, spun up a cigarette, and was licking it into shape when the voice reached him.

"Going somewhere?"

Haslam's head swung and his glance settled, hard and wary. Where he'd been alone a moment before, there was now a man with a gun, who had stepped from behind a point of lava beside the trail. The gun was a rifle, couched across a cradling arm, but with the muzzle bearing steadily on Haslam.

He was lank and lean and young, the owner of the gun. His face was thin and brown, his eyes clear and alert. There was plainly recklessness in him, but nothing mean or shifty. Haslam had met up with a number like him along the back trail. Youngsters selecting the hard trade of saddle hand by choice, yet not long enough at it to be fashioned to some of its grimmer aspects. Haslam relaxed a little.

"They told me in Palisade that this trail would take me to Syl Overdeck's layout."

"Then," decided the young rider, "you could be one of those Ben Spawn brought in with him."

"And if I am?" A thread of harshness showed in Haslam's tone.

"Why, that's fine, and the trail's open," came the easy answer. "Overdeck's been wondering if any of you would show up after last night. Spawn seems to think he had his trip outside for nothing."

"Then Spawn got clear?"

The lean kid grinned. "Yeah. But with considerable of the shine rubbed off. Showed up at the ranch around midnight, his feet blistered from a long walk and his pockets still dripping water from Cold River. I reckon he didn't think it wise to try and get hold of that dun you're riding. I always figured Ben Spawn a little tougher than he's turned out to be. But they do tell me that Hugh Racklyn's got a way of working a man over so that he takes all the fight out of him."

"Depends on the man, maybe," said Haslam briefly. "All right if I move along?"

"Sure! I'll ride in with you."

The young fellow stepped back past the lava point, to ride out a moment later on a chunky sorrel, the rifle scabbarded under his leg. He dropped in beside the dun and said with disarming frankness, "I'm Bud Caddell. Been riding for Overdeck about a year, now."

Haslam said, "Haslam. Riley Haslam."

The trail moved on into the lava badlands and, a little way further along, forked. Bud

Caddell jerked his head toward the left fork. "That one takes you to Deer Creek Meadows and, if you stay with it, clear over Big Saddle Pass. We turn right."

By habit grown solitary and cautious in placing his trust, Haslam found himself instinctively liking this brown-faced youngster. The kid looked at you straight and he talked straight. Back there, when he'd held his rifle on Haslam, there'd been no unnecessary bluster or overburden of threat, nor had there been any lack of quiet nerve. This kid had good wire in him.

Haslam knew he was being covertly studied and he passed a hand across a face still dark with bruises.

"It was pretty rough last night. This Hugh Racklyn and his crowd hit us hard and quick and with plenty. They left a dead man behind, you know. They beat the poor devil's head in."

Bud Caddell caught his breath. "Didn't know that. Spawn said nothing about it."

"Too busy looking after his own skin to care, probably," was Haslam's bitterly dry remark.

They rode in silence after that. The trail worked its way across the badlands, leading ever closer to the towering black barrier of the lava rim. Presently the trail climbed a little rise, then fell sharply down the far side, disclosing another surprise for Haslam's measuring glance. Here ran a well-grassed meadow, probably half a mile wide, reaching some little distance to the north and then a long way to the south, following under the run of the big rim.

Cattle were scattered along the meadow, the sunlight glinting on their markings. On the far side of the meadow, tucked right up against the base of the rim, stood a group of ranch buildings. A narrow line of willow brush, telling of a water course of some kind, came down past the ranch headquarters, angled out into the meadow, then curved south along the main run of it.

Bud Caddell tipped his head. "You're looking at it. The Two Link."

They crossed the meadow at a jog. Haslam, his eyes busy ahead, saw some men at a corral, catching and saddling. One of these headed for the main ranch house, went in. Shortly he reappeared, and with him were two others. A faint shout echoed and two more men came out of the bunk-house, drifted apart with exaggerated casualness, then squared around to wait and watch. Haslam spoke with faint sarcasm.

"Another welcoming committee, looks like."

Bud Caddell shrugged. "It's turned into that kind of country."

Those by the corral said nothing as Haslam and Bud Caddell rode up, though they did give Haslam a careful looking over. Dismounting, Haslam stood for a moment, straightening up carefully against the drag of stiff soreness in his side. A hard-voiced command came across the interval from the ranch house.

"Bring him over here, Caddell!"

The kid looked at Haslam a little uncertainly. Haslam shrugged and nodded. "It's all right."

As they moved on to the ranch house Haslam's glance, ranging ahead, recognized Ben Spawn as one of the three waiting there. In advance of Spawn and the other was a bony, narrow-faced man, who stood with his feet slightly spread. He was deeply swarthy, with coarse black hair that hung straight down in a ragged fringe from under his pushed-back hat. His eyes, black and pebble-hard, bored at Haslam.

"Where'd you gather him in, Caddell?"

"Little this side of the river ford," answered the kid. "His name's Haslam. He's one of those Spawn brought in."

Not even by a nod did Syl Overdeck acknowledge the introduction. He just held his hard stare on Haslam. He got it back, just as hard and just as settled. And he didn't like this. There was an arrogance in this man that expected others to give way before him. He found no giving in Riley Haslam, and under his swarthiness angry color began to build. Haslam's smile was thinly mirthless.

"I've had it tried on me before, Overdeck," he murmured. "The tough stare, I mean. It would mean more to me now if you'd had it and your outfit on hand in Palisade last night to see that Racklyn didn't get away with what he did."

"So-o!" said Overdeck. "Not even signed on yet and trying to tell me my business?"

"Stating an opinion," said Haslam easily. "Habit of mine. I'll say it again. If you'd been using your head, mister, you'd have had Two Link in town last night to even things up a little."

Overdeck's narrow, dark face tightened. "Could be I had it figured like this. Anybody not tough enough to fight his way through wouldn't be tough enough to ride for Two Link."

"That cold-blooded, eh?" Haslam paused, looking the ranch owner up and down. Then he went on bitingly, "A man died in that ruckus, Overdeck. Racklyn's crowd beat his head in. The poor devil hired on with you in good faith, figuring he'd get a fair shake. He didn't!"

As it had been to Bud Caddell, this word was startling news to these men. Overdeck's eyes flickered and he turned to Ben Spawn. "You didn't say anything about that," he charged harshly.

Spawn flushed. "I didn't know anything about it. I had my hands full, with three or four of them piling me at the same time. I didn't have time or a chance to find out anything."

Spawn carried his signs of conflict, all right. His lips were cut and the right side of his face was puffed. There was a heavy, dark welt under his left eye.

Syl Overdeck brought his glance back to Haslam again. "Last night seems to bother you considerable. After it, do you still figure you want to ride for Two Link?"

Haslam shrugged. "That could depend on several things."

"Like what?"

"Wages, for one. I could come a little high, Overdeck. Then there's the matter of where you stand and where I stand. I like to know about such things."

"Last part of that is easy," said Overdeck. "Whoever rides for Two Link stands for

Two Link, all the way. As for wages, we could argue there."

"Not long," said Haslam. "We're not trading horses. I've my own ideas on what my skin is worth. So we dicker on that basis."

"And you figure punching cattle might be rough on your hide?" There was a veiled sneer in Overdeck's words.

Haslam's retort was curtly brittle. "You're talking to a man grown, Overdeck — not to some bald-faced kid. You're not hiring a man like me just to work cattle. I know it and you know it. Suppose we come down to cases. Let's forget the sneer, the strut, and all the other trappings. They're stupid and they don't impress me a bit."

This brought the dark blood again to Overdeck's face. "I could," he said, "tell you to go to hell and send you packing. Which would leave you — where?"

"Wishing you the same, and broke but happy," shot back Haslam. "I think that's the way it will be, anyhow. For the more I see of this Two Link outfit, the less it appeals to me. Particularly the boss."

At the door of the bunkhouse another man appeared. His idly swinging glance touched the group in front of the ranch house, settled there. Suddenly alert, the lazy interest in his eyes sharpened. He gave a muffled exclamation, left the bunkhouse and came swiftly across. Startled words carried ahead of him.

"Riley Haslam! Be damned if it's not — Riley Haslam!"

Haslam came around. Now it was his turn to show recognition and surprise.

"Frank Didion! Drag a stick through the grass and look what shows!"

A grin of pure pleasure split Frank Didion's face as he caught at Haslam's hand and wrung it. Whip-lean, Didion was long-faced, brown and tough as old leather.

"Thought for a minute I was sure seeing things," he said. "Last I heard of you was that you were ridin' on the Skull River range. Somebody or other told me they'd met you there. How'd you get here, Riley?"

"Long story, Frank. Begins to look like I had the trip for nothing."

On closer survey, Didion marked the bruises on Haslam's face. Understanding hit him. "You're one of them Spawn brought in?"

"That's right. And this lop-sided mug of mine is the brand a bucko named Hugh Racklyn put on me. Him and some of his crowd."

"So you're going to ride with us?"

Haslam shrugged. "Figured to, at first. Shaping up different, now."

"Why?"

"Overdeck and me have different ideas on how much I'm worth."

Frank Didion looked at Overdeck. "Better think on it, Overdeck. Riley Haslam is worth plenty. I know. I've ridden with him."

"Capable of making my own decision there, Didion," said Overdeck with thin irritability. Anger was fuming strongly in the man because of the way Haslam had talked back to him. At the same time it was plain that Frank Didion's words carried considerable effect. Overdeck gave Haslam another visual going over, then jerked his head curtly.

"Come inside. We'll talk about it."

# CHAPTER IV

The muted jangle of the cookshack triangle gong brought Janet Wilkerson out of a half doze to full wakefulness. She yawned, stretched slim arms, then pushed herself up on one elbow so that she could look out at the dawning world beyond the open window beside her bed.

Day's first chill grayness held the earth closely here, but way over yonder to the east a ripple of rosy light was beginning to wash along the crest of that grim, black facade which was the Hatchet Rim.

In the cookshack a light was burning and now, drawn by the call to breakfast, the shadowy figures of men emerged from the bunkhouse and drifted across the interval, the voice of one of them a growling murmur against the morning's big silence. The whiff of a rider's first cigarette of the day was a touch of dry, tangy fragrance through the open window.

It was an old and familiar picture to Janet, this first glimpse of a new day, and one she never tired of. But now, as a gust of chill air slid through the window to brush across her bared arms and shoulders, she ducked swiftly back to the snug warmth of the blankets, and considered the possibilities of the day.

Of one thing she could be sure. She'd hear more about last night, both from her father and from her sister Cora. But there was too much of youth's insouciant bounce in Janet to worry greatly over that. Mainly, she decided what the day would hold for her would be a vast curiosity about that man Riley Haslam.

She recalled her first glimpse of him, when he'd stepped down from the train, a tall, solid-shouldered, partially indistinct figure, lugging a sack of gear. She'd had no clear picture of his facial features at the time, yet somehow she'd known there would be ruggedness and strength in them, just as there was a certain suggestion of power in the lift of his shoulders and the cast of his head.

These things she had briefly seen and noted before Hugh Racklyn and his men moved to the attack. After that it had been all turmoil and confusion and the many impacts and sounds of men in physical battle. The thud of driving fists, muffled when to a man's body, but sharper and more crunching when to the open flesh of a man's face or jaw or head. The hard stamp of trampling boot heels. The slithering heaviness of a man's body, driven to the earth with violence.

There had been cries of pain, too, and curses, and the strange seething of a man's pure rage which could be at once a silence, and yet also a vibrancy across the sensibilities louder than any shout. Janet's eyes grew big and sober as she remembered.

For a time she'd lost sight of this Riley Haslam in that wicked ruckus, but then had glimpsed him again, a disheveled, battling figure caught briefly in a gush of light from the suddenly opened door of the station house. And from there she'd seen him lunge off the platform into the night's full blackness beyond.

She was still pretty much at a loss at fathoming her own subsequent moves, when she'd pulled away from her father's restraining hand and circled the station house to locate this man in the dark, somehow knowing that he needed help and needed it desperately. At first he'd snarled at her like some savage, cornered animal, but then he'd accepted her help and guidance to a place of safety.

Later, in Mrs. Orde's quarters in the Staghorn, when he'd thanked her and then asked her why she'd aided him, she'd told him she didn't know, though she was glad she had. And she was still glad about it, if for no other reason than that, in the doing, she had aided and given comfort to an enemy of Hugh Racklyn.

Through the open window beside her now came another drift of fragrance, that of hot coffee, carrying up from the cookshack. Instantly she was hungry and so she was up and dressing swiftly. Going down the shadowy hall to the kitchen she picked up no sound from her sister's room, but beyond her father's door she could hear him stirring.

Dawn was not yet far enough advanced to clear up the gloom in the kitchen, so Janet lit the lamp and then got the fire going in the stove. She washed up, set the coffee on to cook and was slicing bacon when her father came in, scrubbing his hand across his unshaven chin with a dry rasping.

"Yes," said Janet lightly, "the use of your razor wouldn't hurt a bit."

Rufe Wilkerson grunted softly, poured water in the wash basin and then did a great deal of sputtering and blowing as he dipped in. He was a stocky man, with the grizzle of middle age beginning to shade his temples. His features were blunt, his mouth stubborn under a ragged mustache.

Past the muffling folds of the towel he studied this younger daughter of his. All of a sudden, he decided, she'd grown up on him. No longer was she just a leggy kid, full of twinkling deviltry; now she was a young lady who would stand no bullying from anyone, including her father. He'd found that out last night, after she'd come back to him and told him where she'd disappeared to, and what she'd done. He'd started to give her a dressing down for it, only to find himself abruptly up against a quick, flaming dignity that not only silenced him, but astonished and baffled him as well.

Janet, glimpsing her father's almost furtive survey, laughed softly. "Quit peering at me like I was some kind of strange and foreign being. I am still your obedient and submissive daughter."

"Rats!" growled Wilkerson. "You can't soft-soap me. I'm still mad about last night."

"While I," retorted Janet serenely, "am still glad."

There was a gust of real anger in the way Wilkerson threw the towel aside. He caught Janet by the shoulders and turned her to face him and the light. He studied her for a critical moment.

"You really mean that, don't you? You really are glad. And I'll be damned if I can figure why. That fellow you made a fool of yourself over last night — that gunfighter — he's an Overdeck man. You know how I feel about Syl Overdeck. In helping an Overdeck man, you were going against your own father."

"That," Janet said steadily, "is not true. I'd never go against my own father. But I would, and will, go against Hugh Racklyn."

"Same thing as going against me," snapped Wilkerson. "Hugh's my best friend."

A flare of feeling showed in Janet's eyes. "Not your best friend. Your worst enemy. Dad, I don't see how you can be so blind about that man. Or Cora either."

There was a stir at the kitchen door and Cora came in. She was wrapped to the chin in a woolen robe and her bare feet were tucked into a pair of beaded moccasins. Her hair fanned loose across her shoulders, and her eyes were still cloudy from sleep.

"Did I hear my name mentioned?" she demanded.

"You did," said Janet tartly. She pulled away from her father and got busy with the bacon again. Over her shoulder she added, "I was just remarking on how blind you and Dad could be concerning Hugh Racklyn — and how I couldn't understand it."

Cora yawned, patted her lips gently with the back of her hand. "Baby," she said, "I don't mind your not liking Hugh. It's your privilege to like or dislike whom you wish. But please don't try and tell me how I should feel. You're not old enough to possess that much wisdom."

Janet spread a handful of sliced bacon across a skillet, slammed the skillet on the stove with a bang. Nothing infuriated her quite so much as to have Cora use that patronizing, old-sister, all-wise tone and manner.

"I'm old enough to recognize a two-legged brute when I see one," she blurted fiercely. "And that's all I see in Hugh Racklyn — just a greedy, self-centered, two-legged brute."

"Baby, it's too early in the morning to quarrel. But I will, unless you quit calling names." The careless, sleepy indolence that had been in Cora's voice became a sharp brightness.

Rufe Wilkerson, recognizing the signs, spoke up. "Drop it, both of you!" Then he lifted his voice in answer to a knock on the kitchen door. "Come on in, Walt!"

Walt Heighly had been Wilkerson's foreman for the past ten years. He was a solid, dependable, quiet-faced man, and this was a habit of his, dropping in at the ranch house kitchen for a final cup of coffee and to get Wilkerson's orders for the day. He was a neat man, his face clean-shaven and reflecting a weathered ruddiness. His slow drawl, "Mornin'," took them all in, but his glance, as always, lingered longest on Cora. He followed it now with a grave, polite question.

"You have a good visit in White Springs, Miss Cora?"

Cora showed him a quick smile. "The best, Walt. But as always, I'm glad to be home." She liked Walt Heighly, probably because in him she recognized a faithful slave.

With Heighly present there was no further argument, for which Janet was thankful. She finished cooking breakfast, served it up and ate her own in silence. Her father and Walt Heighly were still talking ranch business when she began clearing away the dishes. Cora lingered a little over her final cup of coffee, then went back to her room, looking, thought Janet, almost as pretty in her careless dishabille as when dressed up.

Done with the dishes, Janet went to her room, got her jacket and muffler, slipped out the side door of the ranch house and crossed to the corrals, where riders lounged, waiting for Walt Heighly to show up. Janet singled out one of them.

"Would you catch and saddle for me, Mitch?"

"Sure thing," came the drawling assent. "But ain't you ridin' early?"

"Maybe. But Dad and Cora are mad at me and I think I'm mad at them. It's just as well that I get out from under foot for a while."

Came a chuckle, followed by two words. "Smart girl."

From the ranch Janet rode south, not just riding, but with a destination in mind. The events of last night were still with her and there were things she wanted to know.

The world was growing brighter by the second. Out east, the crest of Hatchet Rim was all afire with the last prelude to full sunrise. Shadow pockets were thinning, beginning to flee before day's advance. The air was cold and keen, sharp-edged against Janet's cheeks. She turned her head to meet the rising sun's first real slashing lance.

It was around midmorning when Hugh

Racklyn, at the head of several of his crew, rode into Palisade. Halfway along the street he pulled up, spoke some orders. The group with him broke up, pulling over and dismounting at the various hitch rails along the street. Racklyn himself rode on to the Staghorn, where he gave a short period of attention to a saddle pony tied at the hitch rail there, before dismounting and tethering his own horse.

In saddle or afoot, there was a brawny massiveness about Hugh Racklyn. He walked as he rode, with a certain challenging arrogance. His features were bold, and in profile carried a predatory cast. His eyes were pale blue and when they flashed in pleasure or anger, it was all surface glitter, with no softer depths showing at all. His lips were long and solidly heavy, marked at the corners with certain lines which hinted of a wildness not always too well controlled. Now he crossed the porch of the Staghorn and entered the door of the bar, his spur rowels spinning, the chains setting up their small clanking.

In the bar, Cash Fletcher was seated at one of the poker tables, poring over a book of accounts. He looked up briefly as Hugh Racklyn entered, then put his attention back on the figures. Racklyn came over to the table, swung a chair around, straddled it, and rested his crossed forearms on the back of it.

"What was the idea, Cash?" The question was flung with heavy abruptness.

Fletcher straightened in his chair. "Idea?"

"You know what I mean. You gave a gunfighter hideout last night. One of Overdeck's gunfighters. Maybe you're nosing in where you got no business."

Cash Fletcher's cigar had gone dead. Now he scratched a match and relit the smoke carefully, meeting Racklyn's look, stare for stare. "Am I?"

The lines about Racklyn's mouth were suddenly deeper. His chair creaked under the stirring of his big weight.

"Lay off the mealymouth, Cash. It don't fool me any. You know what happened last night. You —"

"Yes," cut in Fletcher curtly, "I know what happened. You and your crew murdered a man last night. You beat his head in."

Racklyn's pale eyes pinched down. "Murdered, be damned! It was him or us. But that's not the one I'm talking about. Some of my boys were after another of that crowd. They lost him out back of the Staghorn. They figured he might have gone in the back way. They asked about that and were told he hadn't. Yet this morning that gunfighter was seen with you, coming down those stairs yonder from the balcony. What about it?"

"All right," murmured Fletcher. "What about it?"

"Are you saying you're siding with Syl Overdeck?"

"No, Racklyn. You're saying it."

Cash Fletcher leaned back and hooked his thumbs in the pockets of his vest. The pocket under his right hand held a weighty bulge. His face was as still and impassive as ever, but his eyes were abruptly starkly cold.

"I would tell you something, Racklyn," he said evenly. "I've met with considerable swelled-up arrogance in my time, but your brand of it is the worst I've ever seen. It impresses some, no doubt. But not me. Now get this! Any time I see fit to give someone lodging for the night, that's entirely my affair and none of yours. Suppose you try and remember that."

Their glances locked for a long moment. Then Racklyn's eyes dropped to center bleak attention on Fletcher's right hand.

"That's right," ran Fletcher's even, quiet words. "I got a derringer in this pocket. And I can draw it and use it before you ever got untangled from that chair. So, stay put while I tell you a few more things. Just to keep the record straight, I'm not taking sides with Syl Overdeck. Frankly, I got no more use for him than I have for you. Which is none at all. Because you're damned, greedy wolves, both of you, with no real consideration for a single person but yourselves. I'd like nothing better than to hear that the pair of you had got in a shootout, with both of you ending up ready to bury. This whole stretch of country, with few exceptions, would breathe a sigh of relief and feel that some kind of a dirty fog had been cleared up. Now, does that put you straight as to how I feel and where I stand?"

With the impact of Cash Fletcher's caustic words biting deep, Hugh Racklyn's glance lifted again. The cords in his throat stood out and the surface glitter of his eyes was pale and wild. His heavy shoulders hunched forward and for a moment he seemed prepared to launch himself headlong across the poker table. The muscles along his heavy jaw crawled and worked. Then he settled back and steadied himself with several long, deep breaths.

"All right, Fletcher. That's the way you want it, that's the way it will be. I don't know how well you're heeled for cash, but my guess is that most of it is tied up in this dive of yours. One of these days, maybe, when you watch me and my boys tear it down around your ears, you can remember back on what you've just said to me. Yeah, Fletcher — you can remember it — good!"

Racklyn pushed up and away from his chair, made as if to turn for the door, then spun back half crouched, a swinging hand brushing back and forth past the gun holstered at his side. His words ran harsh, a little thick.

"Care to go for that derringer now, Fletcher?"

Over at the bar, metal bumped wood softly. The bartender spoke, dry and emotionless.

"Two barrels to this one, Racklyn. Both packing buckshot, and looking right at you!"

Racklyn backed slowly away until the range of his glance could take in both Fletcher and the man behind the bar. Over there the twin muzzles of a sawed-off shotgun gaped at him.

"Case game, eh?" he growled. "Might have known it. Never saw a tinhorn gambler yet with the guts to play the cards as they fall. Always wants one off the bottom of the deck. Well, this is just one more thing to remember."

Again he turned to the door, definitely

leaving, now. He was short of it a stride or two when the warped, shuffling figure of Scuffy Elrod moved in from the porch. At sight of Racklyn, he cowered against the wall like a frightened animal. Racklyn passed him without a second glance.

Scuffy Elrod slowly straightened, looking around. Both Fletcher and the bartender were quick to put their glances elsewhere. Scuffy pushed a hand across his furrowed face and hurried into the dining room.

The bartender cursed softly as he tucked his shotgun from sight beneath the bar. "Every time I see Scuffy shrink down that way, I could turn both barrels of this gun loose on that God-damn Racklyn, and bless my luck for the chance." He grabbed a towel and polished the bar fiercely. "Fellow that'd treat another man that way, must have a yellow streak a yard wide."

Cash Fletcher seemed lost in grave reflection. Now he shook his head and spoke quietly.

"Wrong, Pete — way wrong. Hugh Racklyn can be mean as a rattler, cruel as a wolf. But he's got the guts of a grizzly."

Fletcher bent over his account book again and added, almost as an afterthought, "Thanks for stepping in with the bar gun, Pete."

Hugh Racklyn left the Staghorn porch in two long, lunging strides, ridden with a black and seething anger. He headed straight for Sam Basile's office and shouldered his way inside.

Basile sat behind his desk, shoulders dumpy in relaxation. At Racklyn's abrupt entrance he came quickly to his feet, a flicker of nervousness showing in his eyes. Racklyn's words hit out like a club.

"When I got home last night and counted noses, Steg Medill wasn't with us. I figured he'd show up later, but he didn't. This morning, among other things, Clip Parsons brought word that you had Medill locked up. Turn him loose!"

Sam Basile could see the wildness of feeling that was in Hugh Racklyn, so he made his words and tone as soothing as he could.

"I did lock him up for the night, Hugh. After all, I got to make some show of authority around this town. But he's not locked up now. He's free to go whenever he's able to."

"Able to! What the hell do you mean? He didn't get bunged up that bad last night, did he?"

"No, not last night. This morning. Take a look — in my quarters."

There was a rear door to Basile's office, leading through a narrow hall to a jail out back. Part way along the hall a door opened into a side room where Basile slept and kept his frugal personal effects. Here Steg Medill was sprawled on Basile's bunk, a blood-stained bandage around his head. He was only halfway back to a hazy consciousness. Hugh Racklyn, clumping into the room, stared down at his rider, then whirled to Basile.

"What happened to him? You responsible for this?"

Sam Basile shook his head with emphasis. "Not me. That was done by one of the men Ben Spawn brought in on the train. Fellow named Haslam. He took Medill's gun away from him and buffaloed him with it. Buffaloed him, plenty! Hit him twice. Happened right out in front of my office. Doc Jay and me, we lugged Medill in here and Doc fixed up his head. He said Medill would make out all right."

Racklyn stared down at Medill again, then reached over, caught him by the shoulder and dragged him roughly up to a sitting position. "You ready to ride?"

Steg Medill mumbled a little incoherently, still a plenty sick man. When Racklyn let go of him he fell back with a muffled groan. Racklyn cursed his disgust and stamped his way out to the office. Here he whirled on Basile.

"That fellow Haslam — where did he go after buffaloing Medill?"

"He got a horse at the livery barn and headed south out of town."

"How long ago?"

"Couple of hours, I'd say. Maybe a little more."

Racklyn scowled at this. It meant that Haslam was too far and too long gone for pursuit of him to be of any use. Frustration of any kind was something Hugh Racklyn could not stand and now it added more fuel to the biting anger running loose in him. He let it out on Sam Basile.

"Medill wouldn't be in this shape if you hadn't locked him up last night. I figured he was still trying to run down one of Spawn's gang. If I'd known you had him locked up, I'd have kicked in the door of your damned jail and stuffed the keys down your throat. Basile, if you ever lock up another of my boys, that's exactly what I will do to you!"

Basile held his place with shaky stubbornness. "I got authority in this town. There was a man killed last night. You just can't shrug off a thing like that."

"Did Steg Medill do the killing? You got any proof?"

"No," admitted Basile, "no direct proof. But one of your crowd was responsible, and —"

Hugh Racklyn shot out a heavy arm, grabbed a handful of Sam Basile's shirt front, jerked him up close.

"You don't know a damn thing for sure, Basile. It was pretty dark over at the railroad station last night. For all you know, it might have been one of Spawn's crowd who hit that fellow by mistake. But you figured you had to make a showing at your damned job, so you locked up Medill. Well, you've been told. You ever try and lock up another Rocking R rider and I'll run you clear out of the country!"

Racklyn emphasized his final words by giving the marshal a twisting throw which sent him whirling and slamming into the wall. Then Racklyn went out into the street.

Shaken and jarred, Sam Basile stumbled over to his desk chair and dropped into it. The impact against the wall had set his teeth into his lower lip and now beads of crimson slid off the lip and dribbled down his chin. There was no real heat to the day, yet a slime of sweat greased Basile's smooth, dark face. He stared through the doorway at

Hugh Racklyn's departing shoulders, then broke into a low, husky-toned flow of steady cursing.

Out in the street, Racklyn stood for a moment in indecision. Temper was burning in him without letup, and the pale flaring still filled his eyes. He had the feeling that despite what had appeared last night to be a victory in the tug-of-war for power across this range, he had really lost ground. Because he'd missed the man who could, from now on, count a lot. That fellow Haslam.

According to Sam Basile, this Haslam had taken Steg Medill's gun away from him and buffaloed him with it. Now Steg Medill was a tough one in his own right and no ordinary saddle hand was going to get away with anything like that on him. Yet the proof of it was back there in Sam Basile's quarters. There was Medill as Racklyn had seen him with his own eyes, a sick and beaten man.

No, that fellow Haslam wouldn't be an ordinary saddle hand. Instead, he shaped up as a savage, bitter fighter, the sort to pick up other men and carry them along with him, to infect them with some of his own battle ferocity and make them twice as hard to defeat. And Haslam was now riding for Syl Overdeck.

Racklyn set about building a cigarette,

but he tore the first paper and spilled the tobacco. He cursed and set about building another. The sense of having lost ground was
spurring him harder all the time. For this
was spring and beyond Big Saddle Pass the
Silver Glades range would be opening up
and waiting, lush and green and fat for the
first cattle to reach it. Syl Overdeck, he
knew, would be thinking of the same thing.
So it was time to move and to hit hard, if
need be.

Racklyn got his second cigarette into
shape, lit it and took a single deep drag
which burned up the smoke for half its
length. He tossed the butt aside, moved out
into the middle of the street, put two fingers
to his mouth and sent a sharp, blasting
whistle shrilling. All along the street,
Rocking R hands who'd been lounging care-
lessly but, for the most part, watching all
things alertly, turned to the summons and
saw Racklyn's upthrown and beckoning
arm. Two of the riders came out of the
dingy saloon, The Palace, and with the
others collected their horses and came along
the street to where Hugh Racklyn waited.
All of them knew, by the urgency of his
whistle, by the hard sweep of his arm and by
the wild flaring they saw in his eyes that sure
action, and perhaps violence of some kind,

lay ahead. He told one of them off with a jabbing point of a finger.

"You stick around, Shag. When Medill is able to ride, bring him home. He's in Basile's quarters with a beat-up head. Rest of you cut for the ranch. I'll be along pretty quick. We got some cattle to move."

Though all wondered about Steg Medill, nobody asked questions. They knew Racklyn's moods too well and wanted none of his anger. All but Shag, who'd been told to remain, headed out of town in a group. Shag, one of the two who'd been in The Palace, started for Basile's office, hesitated, and turned back.

"Heard somethin' just now, Hugh, over in The Palace. You might be interested."

Racklyn, staring after his reaching thoughts, came around and looked at Shag sharply. "I'm listening."

"It was somethin' Nick Addy heard last night," said Shag. "It was after the ruckus was pretty well over. Nick was headin' for The Palace to take over his shift at tendin' bar. You know it was pretty damn dark last night. Nick come along by the Runnin' W buckboard. Rufe Wilkerson and his two girls were just gettin' ready to leave town, seemed like. And Rufe was mad. He was pitchin' in at the youngest girl — that'd be

Janet, wouldn't it? Anyhow, he was givin' her fits because she'd helped one of the gunfighters Spawn brought in to get away. Nick said he didn't know which one of the gunfighters it was she helped, or just how she helped him. What I've told you is all he heard."

Racklyn considered a moment, then harshly said, "Good enough! But keep it to yourself. Now get in there and look after Medill."

Going down the street to where he'd left his horse in front of the Staghorn, Racklyn swung across and turned into The Palace. Nick Addy was a lank, long-faced one with a high whiskey flush in his cheeks. His eyes were faded, weak-willed, and they fell away uneasily before Racklyn's thrusting glance.

"You just got through telling Shag Bartlow about something you heard last night," said Racklyn. "Well, you've told it far enough. Think of something else to gab about from here on out. Understand?"

"Sure, Hugh," said Addy, "sure — if that's the way you want it."

"That's the way I want it!"

Racklyn turned back to the street. He knew that saddle pony tied at the Staghorn rail, not far from his own mount. For one thing it carried a small Running W stamp-iron brand above the near stifle. For another it was a sorrel gelding that Racklyn had seen Janet Wilkerson upon many times. And now, even as Racklyn stopped beside his mount and began loosening the tie, Janet Wilkerson came around the corner of the Staghorn, pulling on a pair of small buckskin gauntlet gloves. Racklyn's eyes narrowed as he looked at her.

On her part, Janet did not notice Racklyn until she was moving along beside the hitch rail to her pony. She stopped, startled, then faced him coolly. Racklyn made a gesture toward his hat, but never reached it and his lips curled in a sardonic twist.

"Riding kind of early this morning, ain't you, Baby? Maybe you forgot something last night?"

Janet looked him over, making no effort at all to hide her utter dislike of him. She realized that he was sneering at and mocking her. His use of the nickname which her father and Cora had put on her many years ago proved that. From them she did not mind it at all, for from their lips it carried endearment. But its use by Hugh Racklyn infuriated her. This he knew, and was why he used it now.

Janet also knew what he was leading up to, what lay behind his words, and it was characteristic of her that she met the challenge head on. For that matter she never had given, nor would she ever give this fellow the satisfaction of herding her into a single word or act of evasion.

"I wanted to make sure he suffered no lasting effects," she said flatly. "He didn't. They tell me Steg Medill found that out."

The sardonic twist to Racklyn's lips became set. Shadows of that wild flaring showed far back in his eyes. Raw anger became alive in him again. For if he had a way of infuriating Janet Wilkerson, then the opposite was equally true. Others might give way before Hugh Racklyn, but not this girl.

There had never been a time, he thought savagely, when she hadn't opposed him in both manner and words. And always she faced him with a cool and scornful disdain, clothed in a slim, virginal pride that armored her like shining steel. In front of her father and sister he had so far managed to treat her with the calculated indifference one might show a gadfly child. But here, abruptly, anger got the best of him and roughness boiled out.

"So you admit it, eh? That you crawled off in the dark with a damned bought-and-paid-for gunfighter!"

There was grime on the words and more of it on the tone. Janet's spine became a little straighter, her head a little higher. Spots of color burned in her cheeks.

"I wish," she said steadily, "that my father and my dear, deluded sister could have been here and heard you say that. Then they would finally know what I've always known. Which is that behind all the swagger and strut and blow, Mr. Hugh Racklyn is just a cruel, brutish animal!"

She stepped past him then, proud and clean as the wind.

She untied the sorrel gelding, went smoothly into the saddle and jogged off down street to Len Pechard's store, where she again dismounted and tied.

Hugh Racklyn watched her until she disappeared into the store. Then he jerked his own horse free of the hitch rail, hit the saddle heavily and roweled the grunting animal into an all-out run.

# CHAPTER U

The Two Link bunkhouse was no different than a score of others in which, at one time or another, Riley Haslam had lived. Longer than it was wide, one end held a cast-iron heating stove, a roughly round wooden table and several chairs. The balance of the single room was taken up with built-in bunks, ranged against the walls. On one of these, Riley Haslam sprawled full length, resting his injured ribs and thinking his locked-away thoughts.

He'd made his deal with Overdeck, not trying to deliberately gouge the man, but sticking to his demand for what he thought was his just due. Overdeck had given in grudgingly, and by the very manner of his bargaining, had given an index of his make-up.

There was penuriousness in Syl Overdeck, and a coldblooded ruthlessness. He was, as Riley Haslam judged him, a man who would use other men to his own ends with no more compunction or consideration than he would a horse. And when he'd had his full use of them, discard them with no more regard.

In his time, Haslam had ridden for others of similar stripe, so he knew full well what could lie ahead. It wasn't a pleasant prospect and, had conditions been other than they were, he'd have told Overdeck where to go. But a man with empty pockets and on a strange range wasn't always master of his own fate. There were times when he had to take what was offered and make the best of it.

Another thing which a man grew to sense was the all-over temper of a ranch. Even in the roughest of going, some were relatively happy outfits, possessing a certain soundness which bolstered a man's confidence and gave him some feeling of being in the right.

Here on Two Link it was different. Riley Haslam had been at this headquarters some forty-eight hours. In that short time he'd observed a distinct sense of unease about the layout. With the exception of Frank Didion and Bud Caddell and possibly one more, a saddle hand named Tyce Brady, the balance of the crew showed a sort of solitary surliness indicating a lack of confidence in just about every element of the ranch setup.

Outside, on this spring day, the climbing sun was building up a warmth which penetrated the bunkhouse, and under the comfort of it Haslam put aside his moody thoughts and fell asleep. It was nearing midday when he awoke to the pound of a running horse coming in from the north, and he got up and moved to the bunkhouse door. As he reached it, the cook showed at the corner of the cookshack and beat dinner summons on a piece of old iron hung to a wire.

The running horse had come to a stop in front of the ranch house. The rider was Tyce Brady. He dropped off his sweating, blowing mount and hurried to the ranch house door. Syl Overdeck came out and stood talking to him. Responding to the cook's call, ranch hands left off odd chores about the place and drifted toward the cookshack. Frank Didion was one of these and Haslam dropped in beside him.

"Something brewing, Frank?"

"Could be," answered Didion. "Overdeck's had Brady watching the Deer Creek Meadows. Maybe Racklyn's started something over there."

"And if he has?"

Didion shrugged. "We could be riding."

There was an unconscious note of reluctance in Didion's tone which brought dry comment from Haslam.

"I knew a fellow once, named Didion, who figured any kind of a ride was fun."

"That," retorted Didion, "was before he had good sense. He's got some of that sense, now. Not too much, maybe, but a little. He can still find fun in some rides, but not a lick of it in one where he might have to put his hide on the line for an outfit like this one."

Haslam threw a keen glance at his companion. "What's the matter with it, Frank?"

Didion paused, staring out where the Rim towered, black and savage, its presence giving off a distinct impact every time a man looked at it.

"Remember when we rode for Bill Nixon across the old Mogul Bench range, Riley? And for Peck Asbell in North Park? We bumped into plenty of rough trouble in those days. Hard riding, hard fighting. We saw more than one saddle emptied. We helped bury some pretty good men. But somehow things were different, there. Rough as things were, a man had the feeling that he was sitting in a pretty legitimate game. There was something sound and steady about men like Bill Nixon and Peck Asbell. You could depend on them. You knew that when you rode for them they'd back you all the way, come hell or high water. But Syl Overdeck —" Didion shrugged again, shaking his head.

"Yet you're riding for him," pointed out Haslam. "How come?"

Didion looked at him. "You're here, ain't you? Why?"

"That answers me, I guess," admitted Haslam.

"Sure," nodded Didion, "sure! Riley, we learned our trade the wrong way. Being average cow hands didn't drag down enough for a streak of hell that was in our make-ups. We liked the idea of riding where things were a little rougher, and where we got paid extra for our guns. We were young and high-tailed and hell foolish! So we got a brand put on us. Which still wouldn't have been too bad if we'd been willing to drop back to regular wages when the trouble was over. But not us! Hell, no — not us! We were just too damn smart for our own good."

Didion paused, scowled into the distance and went on. "So we went traveling, looking for that extra money. And what did we begin to find out? Why, that regular outfits wanted no part of guys like us. So it got longer and longer between jobs and regular meals. Pretty soon it came to the point where you signed on where you could, and no questions asked by either side. Now you're here and I'm here and if we got our heads shot off five minutes from now, nobody would give a damn, least of all Syl Overdeck. He'd just go looking for more like us to sign up."

"You got the picture pretty straight, Frank," said Haslam. "How long have you been thinking this way?"

"Quite a spell. Mainly since last fall. I'd been with Two Link then a little over a week. A ruckus kicked up between us and the Rocking R. There was a feller named Lyons riding with us. Older feller, nice sort. I liked him. He stopped a bullet. Was Overdeck sorry? Hell — no! He never batted an eye. Riley, fellers like you and me are just something to use and throw away. That's how Syl Overdeck sees us."

Overdeck was now coming across from the ranch house, dark-faced, his black eyes flecked with impatient anger.

"Get along and eat," he ordered roughly. "We got things to do." Turning directly on Haslam, he added some biting sarcasm. "You'll be riding with us. I'm not paying you top wages to lay around the bunkhouse forever on the excuse of a couple of sore ribs."

He would have gone on, but Haslam caught him by the arm. "A minute — just a minute!" Haslam's words were soft, but somehow compelling. "I'll be riding, Overdeck — sore ribs or no sore ribs. And when I hire on with a man I expect to take orders from him and keep my mouth shut, up to a point. But that point is reached when he gives an order more for the sake of a sneer than anything else."

The anger in Overdeck's eyes deepened. "I'm not sure you're going to be with us very long, Haslam."

"Beginning to think so myself," Haslam murmured. "This outfit just don't smell right to me."

Syl Overdeck wasn't used to being talked to like this, not by a hired hand. But neither was he used to being faced with the cool and waiting challenge which Haslam showed him. He stamped on to the cookshack.

Haslam stared after him with some speculation, then spoke softly.

"Streak in that man, Frank. The snarl and sneer are all cover-up."

Frank Didion showed a faintly twisted smile, shaking his head. "Same old Riley Haslam. Ain't changed a damn bit. Won't take a rawhiding from anybody."

"Not unless I got it coming, Frank."

At the door of the ranch house they paused to wash up, then went in and took places at the long, oilcloth-covered table. Syl Overdeck held down one end of it, scowling as he wolfed his food. The crew were equally intent. Another check against the layout, thought Haslam. There was no easy talk, no joshing banter, no comforting relaxation at all. The sourness of disunity was in this room.

Tyce Brady had waited to put his horse up before coming to eat. Now he entered and took his place at the right hand of Ben Spawn, who sat at the lower end of the table. Spawn made some muttered remark, to which Brady shrugged, threw a brief glance at Overdeck, then fell to.

The meal was quickly done with and the men were rolling smokes and beginning to shift restlessly before Syl Overdeck ran his glance around the table and spoke his orders.

"Some Rocking R cattle are feeding in Deer Creek Meadows. We're going over to see about it. All of us."

They left the cookshack, went over to the cavvy corral and began catching and saddling. Ben Spawn, shaking out a rope, had his eye on the line-backed dun that Riley Haslam had ridden out from town. But

Haslam, shooting a deft loop, got there ahead of him. The dun, obedient as soon as it felt the rope, followed Haslam to the corral gate. Ben Spawn came pushing angrily up.

"I'm taking the dun, Haslam. Get your rope off —"

"No!" cut in Haslam. "I rode the horse out of town. Left to you it would still be in the livery corral. So, I'm riding it now."

Spawn rolled up on his toes, his blocky face hard-pulled with anger. His voice was thick. "Mister, you're breeding a hell of a scab on your nose!"

Haslam met the hard stare. "Ben, you don't learn very fast, do you?"

Here it was again, the thing Spawn had seen in Riley Haslam's eyes the first time he'd met him. That cold and brittle something which made men pause and consider. It was something which did not waver, did not give an inch. It whipped Ben Spawn again. He turned away, cursing.

Haslam, as he saddled up, found Frank Didion beside him, cinching his rig on a solid-looking grulla. Didion's murmur was guarded.

"First he faces down the boss and then the foreman. Man, don't you care what you do?"

"Always pays to let some know where and

how you stand," was Haslam's brief answer. "I don't mean to play the bully boy, but there are those who understand only one language."

Others had noted that little byplay between Haslam and Spawn. One of them was the lanky kid, Bud Caddell, who was staring at Haslam with something close to awe. Catching the kid's eye, Haslam smiled faintly. The kid colored and looked away.

Frank Didion, finished with his saddling, threw a glance at Haslam's rig and said, "You're missing something, Riley. Wait a minute."

Didion hurried over to the bunkhouse, came back with a scabbarded rifle.

"Sling this under your leg, boy. That belt gun of yours has its limits, and from what I've seen of it so far, this game we're riding in ain't got any limits. This Winchester belonged to Bob Lyons, that old fellow I was telling you about. He gave it to me before he died. I already got one of my own, so from now on this one is yours. It's a good gun and here's some fodder for it."

Haslam pocketed the cartridges Didion handed over. He pulled the rifle from the scabbard, cracked the action, saw that the chamber was empty, but the magazine full. He slung the rifle under his near stirrup leather and went into the saddle.

They rode north along the Two Link basin range, the Rim pitching up steep and black on their right hand. Cattle feeding in little groups moved aside to let them pass. Haslam's glance touched some of these casually, noting their condition. The Two Link brand was easily read, being the only brand showing on most of the stock. However, there was a considerable scattering of Spoon brands, vented to Two Link.

From the basin they climbed into the same kind of lava badlands the town trail had threaded through after leaving the Cold River ford. Mahogany thickets and scrub manzanita and an occasional lonely pine or fir fighting grimly for existence in a wilderness of upthrust lava fangs and barren, flinty caprock. And always with the dark and forbidding face of the rim glowering down on this hostile world.

Up ahead rode Syl Overdeck and Ben Spawn, and when a twist of the trail put them alone for a moment, Spawn let go some of the simmering anger in him.

"Syl, I'm getting a big bellyful of that fellow Haslam. Just who in hell does he think he is? It's high time he was learning who's giving orders and who's taking them in this outfit."

"Know what you mean, Ben," admitted Overdeck. "But now's no time to raise the point. We got more important things to think about. And I wouldn't be feeling too ambitious about him if I were you. Make no mistake about it, he's a tough one."

"Maybe," blurted Spawn. "But I'm not exactly soft, myself. Next time I give him an order, he'll take it, or I'll damn well find out why, then and there. Either I'm going to ramrod this outfit, or I'm not."

Overdeck threw him a narrow look. "You keep your wolf chained until I say different, Ben. Get me right. I don't like Haslam, myself. But just now I got use for him. Once I don't need him any more, you can do as you please. Throw a gun on him if you feel that salty. I won't give a damn. But until I give the word, you take him and like him!"

Spawn cursed thinly. "I'll take him, but damned if I'll like him."

The Deer Creek Meadows were five in all. They lay in a shallow little valley which funneled down from a break in Hatchet Rim, the break that was Big Saddle Pass. Low, irregular ridges, spiked with lava and brushed with mahogany, pinching in from either side of the valley, made of each meadow virtually a distinct area in itself. The lower meadow was the largest, the other four dwindling in size as they climbed gradually toward the pass. All of them shone with spring's first greenness. Cattle were down there, some thirty or forty head. Most of these were in the lower meadow, a few in the one next above.

Two Link had pulled in on the southern edge of the lower meadow, and now waited Syl Overdeck's verdict in the matter. On his part, Riley Haslam was recalling something that Cash Fletcher had said about the Deer Creek Meadows. Control of these meadows meant control of Big Saddle Pass, and he who controlled the pass also controlled the country which lay beyond Hatchet Rim. That was what Fletcher had said and Haslam saw now how this could be so.

Syl Overdeck sat sideways in his saddle, his narrow face set, his black eyes angry. After his first long look he swung his head.

"More now than when you first saw them, Brady?"

"About the same," answered Brady. "But they were all in the lower meadow then. None had drifted higher up. I can't quite figure this, Syl. If I was in Racklyn's boots, aiming to get control of these meadows, I'd flood them with cows, not just throw in a small jag like's down there now."

"Racklyn's just feeling us out," said

Overdeck harshly. "He's trying out a few head first. If he gets away with that, then he'll throw in more. If he still ain't called, he'll keep on boosting the ante. Well, he's damn well going to be called. We're running those cows out of there. We'll run them so damn far out into the lavas, it'll take Racklyn a month to round them up again."

Riley Haslam, watching and listening, spoke softly. "There's one thing wrong with the picture."

Overdeck threw him a quick hard stare. "Yeah? What's that?"

"I see cattle," said Haslam. "But I don't see any riders. Who'd be fool enough to put cows on a disputed range and not leave a guard?"

"Meaning you're afraid to ride down there?" barbed Overdeck.

Haslam fixed him with shadowed, narrowed eyes. "No, not afraid. I just don't like to be played for a sucker."

Overdeck took another long, searching look at the meadow below. No scene could have been more peaceful. The cattle showed no restlessness, no sign of spookiness or pressure, grazing unconcernedly. Overdeck shook his head, denying Haslam's thought, but confirming his own, stubborn with his convictions.

"I say that Racklyn is just feeling us out, seeing if he can get by with something. If we let him hold two or three dozen critters in these meadows, next thing we know he'll have two or three hundred there. So," he declared flatly, "we're going in. And if you expect to collect any wages, you go in with us." He turned to Ben Spawn. "Take a couple of men and cut up for the second meadow. Get in high and chouse everything down creek. Rest of us go in here."

Spawn indicated two riders and with them spurred away up the little valley edge until they were above the first finger ridge that pinched in from the south. Then they cut over and dropped from sight. Overdeck swung an indicating arm, drawing the rest of the crew with him.

They went in, straight off the valley edge. Haslam let the dun find its own way, while he rode high and loose and ready in the saddle, his glance swinging and searching. The valley cupping the meadows was at its widest here, close to a mile across. So there was nothing to fear from that far rim yet.

But how about the willow thickets along the creek? Or those pinched-in finger ridges above, which, except for a break of a little more than a hundred yards where the creek cut through, separated this lower meadow from the next one above? Some of the cattle were feeding well up toward those finger ridges and a man riding to pick up the cattle would be within easy rifle range of someone hidden there.

They came off the valley slope onto the floor of the Meadow. Again Syl Overdeck waved an indicating arm. "Brady, Didion and Haslam, clean out the upper end. Rest of you make the lower swing."

Tyce Brady obediently moved off. Frank Didion paused long enough to put one sweeping glance all about him, then shrugged and touched his horse with the spur. Riley Haslam moved up beside him and Didion spoke without looking.

"Don't like this, Riley. The cows didn't find their way in here on their own. And like you said, cows on disputed range generally have somebody looking out for them. Just because there ain't no Rocking R riders in sight is no sign they ain't somewheres around. It was a deal something like this one that got Bob Lyons killed last fall. Overdeck just don't seem to learn."

"If trouble's here," said Haslam, "we'll know it before very long. Eyes open, Frank, and be ready to make for cover if something breaks."

Haslam followed his own advice. He circled the cattle and moved them, but the core of his attention was elsewhere. His glance was continually on the move, probing the creek bottoms and the finger ridge to his right. How far to that ridge? Two hundred and fifty, maybe three hundred yards. No more than that, and a man fairly good with a rifle could raise a mean brand of hell at that distance.

Spinning the dun to pick up a two-year-old that had its own ideas of where it wanted to go, Haslam looked down along the meadow. Riders were busy there, circling and bunching. But Syl Overdeck wasn't one of them. Overdeck sat his horse not over fifty yards from where he'd given his final orders. Alone, in the open, and well beyond all reasonable gunshot of any spot of concealment.

The chore of bunching the cattle went on with no sign of opposition. Rope ends slapped bovine haunches and down the meadow one of the riders vented his relief in a shrill yipping. Several head of cattle came into sight through the break in the finger ridges, moving down a trail beside the creek. Ben Spawn and his two helpers were getting results from their end of the job.

Jockeying along the two-year-old he'd gone after, Haslam unconsciously noted the brand, then shot his horse ahead for a closer look. The two-year-old had originally carried a Spoon brand, now vented to Rocking R. For a moment Haslam wondered. He had seen the Spoon iron vented to Two Link. Now it was Spoon vented to Rocking R.

Along with Frank Didion, he moved closer to the creek, while Tyce Brady cut a little higher up toward the finger ridge. With things going well Haslam reined in and Didion did the same.

"Looks like what I expected isn't around, Frank," Haslam said.

Didion let out a long sigh. "For which we give thanks. But Overdeck wasn't too sure you didn't have something there, Riley. Notice where he's staying put? I'd call it taking damn good care of his own hide."

"I've noticed," nodded Haslam dryly.

He got out his tobacco, spun up a smoke. A chunky white face, coming down the creek trail at a trot, broke wide, started to circle back. Tyce Brady was after it immediately, spurring to a run, cutting around and above the animal, which, getting no place trying to dodge back, plunged into the willows and splashed across the creek. Brady stayed with it and, after a short race beyond the creek, turned the critter and sent it racing down the meadow. Then Brady reined up, twisted in his saddle and looked up the creek to see if more cattle were coming through.

Watching, Riley Haslam saw a sudden alertness snap through Tyce Brady, saw him put all his attention on the finger ridge coming in from the north. Abruptly Brady drooped low in his saddle, spurring his horse into a frantic, lunging turn and angled down the meadow at a wild run. Brady's yell of warning lifted, thin and high, and he was dragging at his gun.

Up on the finger ridge a rifle flatly snarled and a gout of meadow sod just ahead and a little to one side of Brady's straining mount, spun away under a bullet's impact. Tyce Brady's yell of warning lifted again, then broke off short as that hidden rifle lifted a second roll of fluttering echoes.

Riley Haslam heard the bullet hit, its impact sodden, muffled. Invisible force seemed to lift Tyce Brady from his saddle, throw him forward along his horse's neck, where he lay for a moment, limp and broken. Then he slithered down, rolled over and over as he struck the earth, shrinking into a huddled, motionless heap.

The cigarette that had formed in Riley Haslam's fingers was suddenly just a drifting wisp of torn paper and a scattered puff of brown tobacco grains. Before the echoes of that second rifle shot had died, he was roweling the dun and sending it at a slashing run straight for the flimsy cover of the willows along the creek. Once he reached this, he swung the dun to the right and raced upstream to the break between the ends of the finger ridges. During this move he hardly noticed the two slugs which snapped past his head.

He hauled the dun to a stop and, as he left the saddle, found Frank Didion crashing up beside him. Didion was cursing wildly.

"That Overdeck! That God-damned fool —" He hit the ground at Haslam's side. "What now?"

"I knew Tyce Brady hardly well enough to talk to," snapped Haslam harshly. "But he was riding with us — and they killed him. Come on!"

While he spoke, Haslam was dragging his rifle from the scabbard. Now he levered a cartridge into the chamber, drove through the willows and across the creek, water foaming about his boots.

This, he thought wickedly, he understood. This was the sort of business he'd cut his eyeteeth on a long time ago. In an affair of this sort there were times when a man was best off in a saddle. But there were other times when he was best off afoot. And this was one of them.

He broke through the willows on the far side of the creek. Here the creek had flung a slight bend to the north and it left Haslam with little more than thirty yards of open to clear before he was under the shelter of the point of the north ridge. He did not hesitate, but went across the distance at a plunging run, with Frank Didion pounding at his heels. It was a gamble, but then, when guns were talking, everything was a gamble. . . .

They gained the ridge point, hugging close to this shelter and working into the first clump of mahogany.

"Shed ten years of my life crossing that damned open," panted Didion at Haslam's shoulder.

They rested a moment, wary and listening. Along the ridge above and ahead of them, gunfire was a steady racket. Out in the lower basin there was answering fire, sporadic and in gusts and pretty distant. Yells lifted, unintelligible and uncertain. Up above, in the second meadow where Ben Spawn and his two helpers had ridden, there was no sound.

Haslam started up the ridge point. It was

rough going. There were lava spikes to climb over and around and brush thickets to work through. Several times there was a bite of pain in his injured ribs, but in his present frame of mind this was a thing far away and of no concern. Close at his heels came Frank Didion. The ridge wasn't very lofty. Soon they were close to the top of the point of it. Haslam slowed, panting thickly.

"You swing left, Frank — I'll take right. Shoot at the first move you see. If this is the kind of music Rocking R likes, let 'em dance to it!"

Haslam circled, gradually edging toward the top. All his senses were straining, reaching out ahead of him. This was the jungle, with stark savagery afoot. He thought of Tyce Brady, huddled and broken and surely dead. This was the old and wicked game of kill or be killed, and there was only one way to play that kind of game.

A rim of lava lifted above him, no higher than his head.

He moved along under it, half crouched. Somewhere out ahead a man called.

"Hodgy — hey — Hodgy! Where'd those two go who cut up creek?"

The answer came startlingly close, from almost directly above Haslam. "Don't know for sure. They put into the willows. I think they're still there. They don't want any of the medicine I gave the first one. I sure centered him on my second try."

"Hell with him!" came the harsh rejoinder. "He's harmless, now. Those other two ain't. So locate 'em. They may be tryin' to get around above us."

A rock grated on other rock, then fell off the low rim not ten feet in front of Haslam. He straightened up, rifle at ready across his body. The head and shoulders of a man lifted past the top of the rim. The fellow's eyes went wide and his lips were a twisted grimace at sight of Haslam. Frantically he tried to swing a rifle into line. Haslam, pulling the trigger of his weapon, thought, "For Tyce Brady, damn you!"

The ringing smash of Haslam's gun was a force which drove the man back and down. Haslam levered another shell home and went on. Up ahead a voice yelled.

"Hodgy, you got 'em spotted? You see 'em, Hodgy?"

Haslam brought his rifle to his shoulders and levered two shots at the voice. They brought a wild bawl of alarm and then there was a crashing of brush as a man threshed his way along.

From the far side of the ridge a rifle gave voice, flat and muffled to Haslam's ears.

Came another startled cry sailing across the ridge top.

"One coming up this side, Pres! Damn near got me —"

Haslam turned straight up for the ridge top, working under and through a thicket of mahogany. Men were calling back and forth along the ridge, and now there seemed to be some confusion and uncertainty here. Reaching the ridge top, Haslam drove a couple more shots, searching the brush along the ridge. A single shot came back, high and wild.

Kneeling, Haslam thumbed fresh cartridges from his pocket, plugged them through the loading gate of his rifle. Then he began working deeper along the ridge. From below and to his left a gun belted the echoes once more.

Haslam called, "Frank!"

Didion's answer came quickly back. "All right! They don't like it this way, Riley."

Ahead of Haslam brush cracked and he glimpsed a running, dodging figure. He snapped a shot and the figure went down spinning. Haslam closed in, ready to shoot again. The man lay supine, stupid with the shock of a smashed arm. All he could do was stare dazedly as Haslam stood over him, rifle poised.

"You!" charged Haslam. "You feeling proud over getting lead into any Two Link rider?"

"No!" came the mumbled, blurted answer. "Not me. I never fired a shot. Hodgy did the killin'. Hodgy started the whole thing. Hodgy did —"

"Hodgy's dead!" Haslam told him coldly. "And you're lucky."

He took the fellow's guns and threw them well out into the brush. "How many of you Rocking R hands in on this deal?" he demanded.

"Six of us to start with. But if Hodgy's dead, like you say —"

"He's dead — plenty!"

Haslam went on. Voices were still sounding out ahead, but more distant now and fading rapidly. Then came the ringing clatter of hoofs on lava cap rock, also fading. By the time Haslam could fight clear of the brush and gain the lift of a lava spike, the ridge was empty.

Sweat streamed down Haslam's face and breath was a hard-earned luxury, running in and out of him with such violence as to bring alive once more the realization of his injured ribs. So he rested and watched, scrubbing the sweat from his eyes.

Frank Didion's hail reached him. "Riley —"

"Over here, Frank!"

Didion came pushing through the tangle, to lean against the base of the lava spike. "Where are they?"

"Pulled out. Had their horses back along the ridge on the east side. Where the hell was Spawn? Had he come in from above, we'd have had the whole crowd on the hip. You do any good?"

Didion spat and swore. "Never got a clear shot, never hit a damn thing. Wanted the worst way to even up for Brady."

"His account's squared," said Haslam briefly. "And there's another back there with a smashed arm. Come on!"

They found the wounded Rocking R rider hunched over, still too dazed and sick to try and move.

"Let's have a look at that arm," Haslam said harshly.

He took his pocket knife and cut away the fellow's sleeve and had his look at the wound. His tone ran a little milder. "It needs Doc Jay if it's ever to be worth much again. Get hold of yourself!"

He managed a fair bandage with the fellow's bandanna, then boosted him to his feet. "This way!"

They came to where a man lay dead and crookedly sprawled atop a low lava rim.

"Hodgy?" demanded Haslam.

"That's him," came the thick, sick answer.

They went on, over and down the point of the ridge and across the short open to the creek. The Rocking R hand flattened out there, plunged his face full under and drank avidly. With his sound arm braced, he pushed back to a sitting position and muttered shakily.

"Gawd — that's good!"

Frank Didion went across the creek and brought back his own horse and Haslam's dun. Haslam said, "You might as well go round up Overdeck and the rest, Frank, and get them here. You can," he added, with black sarcasm, "tell Mr. Overdeck he needn't be afraid. There's no danger, now."

Didion spurred off. Haslam built a cigarette, glimpsed the wounded man eyeing it hungrily, so tucked it in the fellow's lips and scratched a match. The Rocking R hand inhaled deeply.

"Thanks," he mumbled. Then, eyeing Haslam uneasily, he asked, "What'll I get out of this ruckus?"

Haslam built a smoke for himself before

answering. "Nothing worse than you've already got."

"So you say, maybe. But Syl Overdeck and Ben Spawn could have different ideas. Almost sure to."

Haslam shrugged. "It'll be like I say. You're mine until I turn you loose. Then, if you're fool enough to go back to riding for Racklyn again, that's your affair."

A small note of wonder crept into the wounded man's words. "You're a queer one. Damned if I can figger you. You sure finished Hodgy's business for him. And —"

"When I cut down on you I meant to finish yours, too," broke in Haslam harshly. "I just didn't shoot quite as straight as I hoped to. I told you that you were lucky, didn't I? But that part's over with, now."

The wounded one blinked, then sagged back, pain twisting his face. Downstream a little distance came the smash of willow brush and the clack of hoofs on gravel. Syl Overdeck showed up, along with the rest of the Two Link outfit. They came quickly up. Tyce Brady's horse was working uneasily along the edge of the willows still further down and Frank Didion, swinging that way, picked up the animal and brought it along.

Riley Haslam watched Syl Overdeck with shadowed eyes. He saw the Two Link owner flash a quick, fleeting glance at the still figure of Tyce Brady, then bring it around and settle it on the wounded Rocking R rider as he came riding up. The rider, humped and sick, tipped a somewhat fearful look at Overdeck.

"Cory Biggs!" said Overdeck thinly. "He responsible for — Brady?"

"No!" said Haslam bluntly. "You are!"

Overdeck, who'd been leaning forward in his show of arrogance, settled back in his saddle, his narrow face dark in the sun. "Just what the hell do you mean by that, Haslam?"

"What I said. You heard me. You're responsible, you and Racklyn. In this case, you particularly. I tried to tell you things didn't look right down in this meadow. But you wouldn't listen. So now, Tyce Brady is dead."

"Too bad, of course," said Overdeck. "But any man in the saddle must take his chances."

"Any man but you," retorted Haslam sarcastically. "Isn't that what you mean, Overdeck? I noticed you kept well back, beyond rifle shot. You left it up to a poor damn fool of a hired hand to ride in and get it. You just don't take any chances, do you, Overdeck?"

At Overdeck's side, Ben Spawn stirred angrily. "Haslam, your mouth gets bigger and bigger. Watch it!"

Haslam fixed him with a cold, steady stare. "Now I wondered about you, too, Spawn. You were supposed to be in the next meadow up. A perfect place to flank that ridge where Rocking R was laying out. But when the shooting started there wasn't sign or sound of you. What was wrong? Couldn't you make your bronc head that way?"

Spawn's little, heated eyes wavered, dropped to Cory Biggs. "I don't know of a better time and place to even up for Tyce Brady," he said thickly.

"You can forget that kind of talk," Haslam told him. "This man belongs to me. You leave him alone!"

"Leave him alone, be damned!" stormed Spawn. "After the other night at the railroad station, and now this here business —" He waved a clenched fist. "I've had a big bellyful of Rocking R. From now on, far as I'm concerned, any Rocking R rider is fair game, any time, any place. Like now. This Biggs gunned Tyce Brady. So —"

"He didn't," cut in Haslam curtly. "The fellow who gunned Brady was known as Hodgy. He's dead — back up on that ridge. I tell you, Biggs is mine. Nobody touches him without my say-so. Now if you were so damned starved for a bite at some Rocking R hide, all you had to do to get it was to go up on that ridge along with Frank Didion and me. What was holding you back, anyhow?"

Searching for an answer, Spawn swung his badgered glance around. Among others, he saw the kid, Bud Caddell, watching him, and there was a distinct and sardonic curl to the kid's lips.

"Still wondering, Spawn," probed Haslam mercilessly. "What was holding you back?"

Open bluster broke from Spawn. "I was plumb at the top of the second meadow when the ruckus opened. It was done with before I could do any good."

Haslam's laugh was short and mirthless. "Of course, of course! You were way up there, while Overdeck was way back yonder. I've the feeling that's how it will always be with this outfit when the going gets tough. That's why I want no part of it any more. Why I'm calling quits, right now!"

"So that's it, eh?" said Overdeck. "A little rough stuff and you're through. While Didion here had me partially sold on the idea that you were tough!"

"I did — and he is," put in Frank Didion. "I say it again."

"Yet he's quitting," taunted Overdeck. "Why?"

"Well," said Haslam, "I'll tell you, Overdeck. I'll try and make it real plain, so there's no chance for a mistake. It's like this. I might ride for a man who was a fool. I might even ride for one who was a coward. But I want no part of one who's both! Now, is that plain enough and reason enough?"

Rage in Syl Overdeck was a sudden throbbing at his temples. His eyes went dead black and his lips thinned to a bloodless line, barely moving as his words seeped out.

"Haslam, you're getting a long way out on a limb!"

"If he is," said Frank Didion quickly, "just figger that I'm right alongside of him. I went up on that ridge with him. I seem to have got the habit."

This flat statement left Syl Overdeck hanging in mid-air. If he tried to push this thing to a showdown, would the rest of his riders back his hand against Haslam, or would they do as Frank Didion had done, step over to the other side of the line? Haslam saw the uncertainty working in Overdeck — and smiled thinly.

"Thanks, Frank," he said. "I think that settles it. Give Biggs a hand-up on Brady's bronc. Tyce won't need it any more and that arm of Biggs's needs a doctor. We'll take him to town."

"Not on a Two Link bronc, you won't!" shrilled Overdeck.

Haslam squared himself, staring at Overdeck fixedly. He spoke ever so softly. "We'll see. Go ahead, Frank!"

Cory Biggs stumbled to his feet and, with Frank Didion boosting him, made it into the saddle of a man but lately dead. Haslam and Didion stepped astride.

There were any number of things Syl Overdeck would have liked to do. There was nothing he dared do. These two gaunt, hard-faced men before him sat awfully tall in their saddles about now. And, no matter what his personal feelings in the matter, he couldn't deny the cold facts, at least to himself. These were the two who had gone up on that ridge together to shoot it out with Rocking R. No amount of surcharged feeling could afford to ignore a fact like that.

"All right, Frank," said Riley Haslam. "Head out!"

And so they rode away, Haslam and Didion and the wounded Rocking R hand, Cory Biggs.

# CHAPTER UI

Afternoon shadows were beginning to form along the street of Palisade. These first good days of spring had stirred life of all kinds into movement. Several of the smaller ranchers from down in the Ash Pan Flat district and from the more distant Burney Basin had driven into town and their rigs, buckboards and spring wagons, stood along the various hitch rails, particularly crowded in front of Len Pechard's store.

Some of the owners of these rigs, waiting their turn in the store, had gathered on the porch, trading frugal talk of their several affairs with a certain guarded attitude which told that they were not entirely at their ease here. On a corner of the porch a nondescript black and white dog sprawled, yawning and watching the street with sleepy eyes. Back in the timber beyond the railroad station and yards, a flock of ravens discussed nesting problems in harsh, discordant tones.

Drawing leisurely on a cigar, Cash Fletcher stood in the doorway of the Staghorn, where presently he was joined by Dr. Jason Jay. The big redhead ran his glance along the street.

"Seems good to see those Ash Pan Flat and Burney Basin folks in town again," he rumbled. "They don't show very often."

Fletcher removed the cigar from his lips, flicked the ash off it before answering soberly.

"They never will, so long as Racklyn and Overdeck keep things at a tension. Those folks are here for just one purpose, which is to stock up with flour and other grub and a few necessary odds and ends. Chances are we won't see them again for two or three months, when their grub runs low again; and if there was another source of supply within reasonable driving distance, we wouldn't see them at all."

"Town," observed Doc Jay thoughtfully, "should mean more to a country round about than just a place to slip into now and then for a wagonload of grub."

"When you say that, Doc, you're talking my language," said Fletcher with quiet emphasis. "Town should be a place where lonely ranch women could get together every once in a while with others of their kind, to gossip and make small talk and do the kind of visiting dear to a woman's heart.

It should be a place where they ain't afraid to bring their kids, where those same kids could play and yell and chase one another around, where they could look and marvel at things in store windows and spend a nickel or two for some hard candy to chew on. This could be that kind of a town, but it's not that kind now and it never will be while Hugh Racklyn and Syl Overdeck hold the country by the throat, snarling and biting at each other."

Doc put his glance fully on Fletcher. "I know you pretty well, Cash. But every now and then I discover something more in you to startle me."

Fletcher shrugged briefly. "Long ago, Doc, I learned a trade. In the eyes of a lot of folks it's not a very good trade, and maybe they're right. If I had it to do over again, I'd probably do different. But it's too late to change now, so I make the best of it. Somebody has to run the bars and gambling houses. As long as I'm running one, I aim to make it a decent place and to keep it so."

Fletcher's cigar had gone out. He paused to run a match across the tip of it. Then, through a mouthful of smoke, he went on.

"You ever see a man get drunk at my bar, Doc? No, you never did, and you never will. And you never saw a man lose more than he could afford to lose over one of my tables. This is my town. I like it. I aim to stay here. Before I'm done, all fair-minded people are going to respect me and the place I run. I like most people and I want them to like me."

Down at the southern end of the street there was a stir of movement and the soft mutter of hoofs. Doc Jay craned his neck and exclaimed:

"Haslam — and a couple of others, Cash. And from the way one of them is hunched over, he's a damn sick man!"

The riders came steadily along, pulling to a stop in front of the Staghorn. Riley Haslam nodded briefly.

"Gentlemen! Doc, I was hoping to run into you. For here's a man with a pretty bad arm."

Doc Jay wasted no time in asking questions. "Bring him over to my place," he said.

Haslam and Frank Didion got Cory Biggs out of the saddle and steadied his faltering steps. He'd made a pretty game ride of it, considering.

Doc Jay's place was made up of three rooms at the corner of the building next to the Staghorn. Doc, after a quick, keen glance at Cory Biggs, began rolling up his sleeves and indicated a table. "Spread him out on that."

They eased Biggs down and Doc scissored away the bloodstained shirt. He made swift examination, then reached for a probe. At the first touch of this, Cory Biggs grunted and went completely limp.

"Out," growled Doc. "Just as well. Save him a lot of misery if he'll just stay that way until I get through with him."

Doc worked swiftly, his big hands amazingly deft and sure, and he made rumbling comments now and then.

"I've seen worse, but this is bad enough. This wing isn't going to be much use for a while. Who gave it to him?"

"I did," said Haslam.

Doc grunted. "Humph! Warmed up to the job quick, didn't you?"

Haslam shrugged. "Syl Overdeck let us into something. Biggs, here, was lucky. I can name you two dead men."

"That," declared Doc, with emphasis, "would be fine if you'd name Overdeck and Racklyn."

"No such luck. Two Link lost Tyce Brady. Rocking R, a fellow called Hodgy."

Doc swore feelingly. "It would be that way. It's always that way. Always the hired hand. They come fairly cheap. Somewhere they die! So you bury one and you hire on another. . . ."

Cory Biggs was still out when Doc finished. Doc jerked an indicating nod toward an inner room. "Bunk in there. Put him on it. For a few days he's not going to feel exactly like pushing a mountain down. I'll get word to Rocking R to come and collect him when I think he's ready to move."

So they carried Cory Biggs into the inner room, pulled off his boots and put him between blankets. When they came out, Doc, who was cleaning instruments, put a sharp glance on Haslam.

"Still like your job?"

"I got no job," said Haslam. "Me and Syl Overdeck just couldn't get along."

Doc smiled broadly. "Fine — fine! Tell Cash Fletcher that."

"Why should I?"

"Tell him and see."

Cash Fletcher still stood at the door of the Staghorn. He watched gravely as Haslam and Frank Didion came back from Doc Jay's quarters. Halfway to the Staghorn, Haslam paused.

"Frank," he said, "what's to do about you? I sure appreciate the way you sided me, but I'm sorry to drag you away from your bed and board."

Didion shrugged. "Don't be. The way things broke just made up my mind for me. I never was what you'd call happy, out at Two Link. About time to drift, anyhow."

"Makes a pair of us then," said Haslam. "I got enough to buy a drink. Come on!"

They dragged their spurs along the Staghorn porch. To Cash Fletcher, Haslam said, "Frank Didion and me, we're having a farewell drink before we head out across the mountains. Have one with us, Cash. I owe you one."

Cash Fletcher was still for a moment, though a quick light flickered briefly in his eyes. Then he silently nodded and followed them in. Not until they were lined up at the bar did he speak.

"You just said you were going to head across the mountains. Does that mean you're free agents?"

"Right!" said Haslam succinctly. "Free as the wind. And as uncertain, just now."

"Of course I'm wondering why," Fletcher said. "I thought you were all set to ride for Syl Overdeck."

"So did I, for a while. Not now. I just don't like the way friend Overdeck operates. Too much a deal of your skin and his profit."

"Hasn't it always been that way, more or

less? Along the back trail, I mean?"

Haslam, staring at the glass with sudden stillness, nodded slowly. "To an extent, yes. But not quite as barefaced as with Overdeck. Again, like Frank had suggested earlier today, maybe I'm just beginning to get some sense. Anyway, here's whiskey!"

He lifted his glass, tossed off the drink.

Fletcher quickly motioned the bartender to another fill. "On me," he said. He looked at Haslam. "The other day, if you remember, I made some reference to a deal that might interest you, when and if you got a bellyful of Syl Overdeck and his ways. Care to hear about it?"

Haslam looked straight ahead, his eyes pinching down. He answered slowly, his tone almost somber.

"Cash, I don't know. When I cut loose from Overdeck a little while ago, the thought hit me that now was the time to cut loose from a lot of things. It hit me of a sudden that I was at the forks of a trail, and that I'd never stand at the same forks again. It was a case of now or never. I looked at Tyce Brady and decided right then that no ante of straight wages, no matter how big, would ever be enough to hire me again without plenty of principle to back them up.

A man should have more to die for than just — wages."

"Ho!" exclaimed Fletcher softly. "That I've been waiting to hear. What I'm thinking of means a lot more than just wages. Care to listen?"

Haslam shrugged. "I'll listen. But not promising a thing, understand."

"That's the way it should be," Fletcher agreed. He paused to light a fresh cigar. "Do you recall what I told you about Scuffy Elrod and the Deer Creek Meadows?"

Haslam's glance came around. "Scuffy Elrod? That's the old fellow who got all broken up when his horse dragged him?"

"That is the explanation commonly accepted in some quarters," Fletcher said dryly. "Doc Jay and I have ideas of our own on the subject which may or may not be correct. At any rate, Scuffy still owns the Deer Creek Meadows range. As you saw for yourself, he will never be able to work that range again. What happened to him wrecked him physically and, to some extent, mentally. Yet there is enough value tied up in the Deer Creek Meadows, in what they once were and in what they could become again if realized upon, so Scuffy would never lack for money to get along on for the rest of his life. What Scuffy needs is a partner, the right kind of partner, to take over on a fifty-fifty deal, straight across the board."

"And you're suggesting that I be that partner?" Haslam asked.

"That's right," said Fletcher quietly. "Understand, I'm not making this offer on my own responsibility and authority. It's something I've talked over several times with Doc Jay and Len Pechard. They're both sound, responsible men. You might say that we've set ourselves up as a committee of three to look after Scuffy's affairs for him, now that he's no longer capable of looking after them himself."

Haslam toyed with his glass. "I might suit you as a choice, Cash — but how about Doc and Pechard? They may feel different, Pechard in particular. For I've never even spoken to the man."

"You've been talked over among the three of us," Fletcher admitted. "Like me, they're hoping you'll be interested."

Again Haslam stared at nothing, his eyes narrowed. "Even if I was, I couldn't swing it, Cash. I'm as close to being flat busted as a man can get. I got no money to put up as my share."

"That angle doesn't enter at all," said Fletcher quickly. "You got something to offer which is needed far more than money.

You got yourself, to take over that range and hold it against Hugh Racklyn and Syl Overdeck. You do that, then you more than earn your full right to half of it. Otherwise, Scuffy stands to lose all of it."

"Empty range don't mean a thing, Cash. You got to have cattle on a range to make it worth anything."

"There were cattle and there will be cattle," Fletcher stated flatly. "At the time of Scuffy's trouble there were between two hundred and fifty and three hundred head of cattle on that range. From what I've heard, they aren't there now. I've heard it said that most of them worked up through Big Saddle Pass and out into the Silver Glades country beyond. It's big country, so I understand, in which cattle could scatter — far."

Fletcher took a deep drag on his cigar, then went on, a caustic note creeping into his tone. "I've also picked up hints of stories less flattering to the allover honesty of the country round about. I'll not repeat these stories because a smart man doesn't make that kind of talk unless he's got proof. At any rate, maybe the trail of at least some of the cattle can be run down. If not, there'll be money to buy more."

Riley Haslam went into another period of

silent, brooding thought. In spite of the depressive mood that had held him since the shootout at Deer Creek Meadows, now a stir of interest wakened in him as he considered the promise and possibilities of Cash Fletcher's proposition.

It wouldn't be easy, this thing that Fletcher was offering. It would be anything but easy! Still, what was there really worth while in the world that ever came easy? He swung his shoulders and his head came up again, his glance probing at Fletcher.

"As long as we're putting everything on the line, Cash, I got to ask you this, knowing human nature for what it can be. I asked you something of the same thing before and I never got a full answer. I want one now. What else do you figure to get out of this besides a square shake for Scuffy Elrod? You must have a personal stake in it somewhere."

"I have," Fletcher admitted calmly. "So has Doc Jay and Len Pechard. So have all other decent folks, all along this stretch of country. It's a good country and Palisade is a good town, but both could be better. Yet neither ever will be, so long as Hugh Racklyn and Syl Overdeck spread their damn feud across it. So, bluntly, in you, Doc Jay and Len Pechard and I think we see a man who can cut the combs of Racklyn and Overdeck. We realize it can work out as a pretty rough chore, but we're not asking you to do it for nothing, or for wages either. We're offering you something really worth while. It means a fight, but you'll be fighting for yourself, not somebody else. So there it is. You got all of it, now."

Riley Haslam sifted tobacco out of a muslin sack dangerously close to complete flatness. Here he was, at the forks of that trail again. One fork led nowhere that he could foresee. But the other did lead to something real, something he could get his teeth into. It wouldn't make soft chewing, but it was something a lot more than just wages and nobody giving a particular damn. Then there was a certain amount of principle there, maybe a lot of it when he got it all thought out. How much thinking about it did he need? Time wouldn't change the facts, so where was the sense of wasting time?

He tapered up his cigarette carefully, lit it, then motioned toward the bottle.

"I'll have one more. I'll probably need it. For I'm taking you up, Cash. If you think I'll do, I'm your man."

Fletcher stuck out his hand, the widest smile Haslam had yet seen on him, now showing. "Shake! I got a feeling about this, Riley. A good feeling!"

Silent up to now, Frank Didion stirred and said, "Looks like I'll be riding across the mountains alone. Good luck, Riley!"

"No!" exclaimed Haslam quickly. "No, Frank. You're not riding across any mountains alone. I know my limits. This chore ahead is anything but a one-man job. I'm going to need fellows like you. And I rate some outfit, don't I, Cash?"

"Of course!" said Fletcher heartily. "Sign him on, Riley. I like his looks."

Frank Didion stared at them gravely. "You really mean this?"

"Every damn word," asserted Haslam. "You went up on that ridge with me. You went out on the limb with me. Now you go along with me here."

Frank Didion drew a deep breath, pushed out his glass. "Then I'll get in on the drink. It would have been damned lonesome, ridin' across the mountains by myself."

As they drank, then turned away from the bar, Haslam said, "Elrod must have had a headquarters of some sort. Wonder is it still there?"

"So far as I know, yes," said Fletcher. "That, I imagine, will be your first move. To go in there and take possession. You'll need supplies and all that sort of thing. Anything like that, you can call on Len Pechard for."

"Yeah," nodded Haslam. "First move is to set up our headquarters and let it be known the meadows are private range. Then we'll start looking for some of the cattle Elrod had. By the way, Cash, what brand did Elrod use?"

"A simple one," said Fletcher. "The Spoon."

They had been moving toward the door of the Staghorn. Now Haslam stopped abruptly. "Say that again, Cash."

Fletcher looked at him with some surprise. "Why — sure. The Spoon. What about it?"

"Maybe — plenty! Did Scuffy Elrod ever sell any beef to Syl Overdeck — or to Hugh Racklyn?"

Frank Didion exclaimed softly. "I get you, Riley," he said. "I get you. I've seen that vented brand. Yeah — I get you!"

"I wouldn't mind getting in on the mystery," said Fletcher dryly.

"No mystery, Cash," Haslam said briefly. "Only, I've seen a Spoon brand vented to Two Link, and I've seen a Spoon brand vented to Rocking R. And unless Scuffy Elrod sold or traded those cattle to

Overdeck and Racklyn, we've got something ahead that could turn interesting, very interesting!"

"Well, now," murmured Fletcher, "damned if it couldn't."

The cabin that had been Scuffy Elrod's headquarters stood in the middle meadow of the five, close to the north side of Deer Creek. There was just the cabin, a small gear shed and a couple of pole corrals. The corrals and gear shed were pretty far gone, but the cabin, more stoutly built, wasn't so bad. Even so, there was plenty to be done to make it reasonably livable. The two glassed windows were both smashed out, and one hinge of the door had been wrenched loose, so that the door hung askew and would not close.

The stove was rusty, but still sound. There were a couple of short benches and a rough table, and two bunks were built against the walls. In the middle of one of these a family of pack rats had built a heaped-up nest of twigs and grass and leaves, and there was a wild scurrying as Riley Haslam and Frank Didion pushed past the sagging door. Haslam squinted through the gloom.

"Seen better — and worse," was his brief

comment. "Considerable mucking out to do, but it's not as bad as I figured it might be."

Frank Didion nodded, grabbed up the stub of an old broom and took a fruitless swipe at a scurrying pack rat that whisked from under a bunk and darted for the door.

"Git, you thievin' son of a gun!" grunted Didion. He looked at Haslam, grinning. "We fix that door and those windows, Riley, or that one and all his relatives will rob us blind. Ha! There goes another one!" Didion threw the broom stub at this fleeing rodent but had no success there, either.

Haslam took another look around, mentally cataloging the needs of the place, then stepped outside and spun up a smoke, while laying a long, speculative glance all about him.

Sundown was at hand and pools of thick violet and coldly blue shadow were flowing and swelling everywhere, and already this shadow was a tide washing at the base of Hatchet Rim's grim and forbidding bulwark. Way up there where the highest of the five meadows broke against the grim façade of the rim, the shoulders of barren lava rock which framed Big Saddle Pass were caught in the reflected glow of sunset and stood boldly clear above the ever widening and deepening sea of shadow.

At closer hand, north and south, lay the run of this middle meadow, filled with the quiet serenity of approaching dusk, the only sound being the subdued murmur of water in the creek. He had, mused Haslam, seen his share of country across a score of different ranges, some of it fat land, some of it hungry land. None of it had ever held any special significance for him; country was just country in the eyes of a man driven with restlessness and the urge to move on and on. He had ridden hard across it, worked across it and, at times, fought across it, and so left it behind him with no particular care, and certainly with no regrets.

Perhaps this had been so because he'd never actually owned any part of it. Never had there been a piece of ground on which he could plant a foot and say, "This is mine!" Always he had been just the hired man, never the owner. But here was the chance to change that. Would it be worth the effort?

Yes, he'd seen lots better range than this. For this was rough country, hostile country. A man who managed to build a living out of this country would earn every thin dime of it. Here was challenge all the way, not only from the land, but from those he'd have to battle for the right to own this land.

All these half-formed doubts ran through Riley Haslam's mind, making their individual impact, then bouncing off the armor of a strange contentment which had settled upon him. This, he abruptly knew, was his land, like no other land had ever been before, like no other land could ever be. Here, after so many years of drifting and wandering, he had come home. This conviction wasn't fancy. It was the most conclusive certainty he'd ever known.

He stretched his arms, arched his chest, flinched slightly at the reminding twinge of his ribs. But still he breathed deep and spoke with exultation.

"It took a long time over a hell of a mixed-up trail to get here, Frank. But here I am, and here I stay. We'll come back in the morning and set up housekeeping, now that we know what we need."

It was full dark by the time they got back to Palisade.

They ate late supper in the dining room of the Staghorn. Before they had finished, Doc Jay came in, pulled up a chair and gave a rumbling-voiced report on his patient Cory Biggs.

"Be the best part of a week before he'll be able to stand the ride out to Rocking R headquarters. And there's a man who can't figure you at all, Haslam."

Haslam met Doc's glance. "How's that?"

"You could have killed him, and you didn't. Then, so he tells me, you faced down Overdeck and Ben Spawn because of him and, finally, you brought him in to me to be fixed up. All these facts got him fighting his head. And with some reason, I got to admit. I'm curious enough to ask — why?"

"You said it yourself, Doc, when you were working on him. Just another hired hand, the same as I was myself. He happened to be on the other side. But he didn't think up the trouble. Somebody else did. They were the ones responsible, not Biggs."

"You didn't feel that way when you pistol-whipped Steg Medill," reminded Doc. "Yet, he was just another hired hand, too."

Haslam's face darkened at the memory. "Different there, Doc. Medill had done his damnedest to stamp my ribs in, to kick me to death. That made the issue personal. But when I cut down on Biggs, he was just an impersonal shadow, dodging through the brush. If he'd shot at me, then he'd have seen me in the same way. There may be some distinctions there which don't make sense to you, Doc. But they do to me."

"Maybe," said Doc, "I understand pretty well, at that." He switched to a more pertinent subject. "Fletcher gave me the good news. You're taking over the meadows?"

Haslam nodded. "Having a try at it." He leaned back, spun up a cigarette, fixed Doc with a settled glance. "Because of this and that, plus some lack of high opinion of the human race in general, I'm wondering about something which you can probably put me nearer right on than anyone else. You took care of Scuffy Elrod after he was hurt?"

"That's right, I did. And I must say that for considerable time I never thought I'd bring him through alive. What's about it that you want to know?"

"He was supposed to have been dragged by his horse?"

"No suppose about it," said Doc. "He was dragged." Now Doc met and held Haslam's glance very directly as he added softly, "But it was strange, very strange."

"In what way, Doc?"

"Maybe," said Doc, "I better start at the beginning. Scuffy Elrod was found by Hoopa Joe, a half-breed government hunter. Hoopa Joe had come in over Big Saddle Pass, heading for town here for some supplies. Riding down through Deer Creek

165

Meadows he ran across this horse wandering along, saddle empty, but with a man dragging beside it, one foot caught in a stirrup. The man was Scuffy Elrod. At first Hoopa Joe thought Scuffy was dead. Then he saw that Scuffy was still breathing. So he cornered the horse, got Scuffy's foot free and came after me as fast as he could travel."

Doc traced an aimless pattern on the table top with a big forefinger, frowning as he recalled these things. "I'd treated men before who'd been dragged, so I knew there'd be broken bones. I got a couple of extra horses and some help and headed for the meadows. We fixed a blanket stretcher between two horses and brought Scuffy to town that way."

Again Doc paused and Haslam said, "What's so strange about that, Doc? Sounds pretty cut and dried to me."

"Doesn't it?" murmured Doc. Then his voice deepened, became a growl. "And it would have been except for the fact that there were marks of violence on Scuffy Elrod that he never got by being dragged. I know my fractures, my cuts and abrasions; I know intervals of time and distance. So, I know that Scuffy Elrod had been savagely beaten before he was dragged, and that in all probability he was unconscious during the time he was dragged. On top of that, I know what Hoopa Joe told me. It was something that had Hoopa Joe deeply puzzled."

"Still listening, Doc," murmured Haslam. "What was that?"

"Why," explained Doc, "Hoopa Joe couldn't understand why Scuffy Elrod's right foot should be tangled in the near stirrup. Neither could I. Can you?"

Haslam sucked hard on his cigarette, ground the butt out on the edge of his plate. "Who'd be stupid enough for a trick like that?"

Doc's answer was dry. "People contemplating murder, ridden by the guilt complex and fearful of discovery do many stupid things."

Haslam nodded slowly. "It's a trick that's been tried before. Beat a man half to death, or entirely so, then hook his foot in a stirrup, chouse his horse to a run, and figure the result will cover up the crime. No doubt there have been times when it has. You've questioned Scuffy about it? He must certainly know who it was that gave him the beating?"

Doc leaned back, steepling his finger tips. "I tried to get it out of him. I put paper and pencil in front of him, asked him to write down the name or names of the man or men. Scuffy can't talk, you know: the beating left him a mute. It left him with other lasting effects, too, which may not make sense to the layman, but which do to medical science. When reminded of that day, things go all out of kilter for Scuffy, and he is not responsible with his conscious reactions. His instinctive reactions, however, are a different matter."

"You're suggesting something, Doc," Haslam said. "What is it?"

"Like this," said Doc. "You're going to take over in the Deer Creek Meadows, so you've a right to all I know. And I know this. I know that on three different occasions, when Hugh Racklyn happened to be passing close by, I've seen Scuffy Elrod cower and cringe. And I have never seen him act that way around any other man!"

# CHAPTER VII

Nate Foskett, station agent at Palisade, was a paunchy, placid, red-faced man, entirely content with his job and wanting nothing better. His duties were light — only one train a week making the round trip in from White Falls Junction, excepting an occasional cattle special, when the shipping season was on. A bachelor, with living quarters in one end of the station building, Foskett got by comfortably on his meager salary, with enough cushion for a fairly liberal whiskey allowance per day.

Come evening, with the chill of night setting in, there was nothing Nate Foskett liked better than a whiskey toddy of his own special mixing, spiced exactly right with cinnamon and cloves. He was mixing one this night when Riley Haslam came in at the business end of the station and filled the wicket with a pair of big shoulders. Disgruntled at the interruption, Foskett's scowling question was hardly civil.

"Well? What is it?"

Haslam did not answer for a long moment, just looking at Foskett with a penetrating steadiness. Foskett began to squirm, the floridness of his face deepened, he blinked and his glance slid away. He cleared his throat and his tone ran milder.

"Something I can do for you, mebbe?"

"Better," murmured Haslam, "much better. Yes, there is. You can give me some straight answers to some straight questions. Rocking R and Two Link have both shipped beef through this station at times?"

There was just a hint of wariness in Foskett's nod. "Of course. Every cattle outfit this side the Chevrons for a hundred miles around ships through here. Close in, there's Rocking R, Two Link, Running W. From down below Ash Pan Flat there's Arrowhead, and in the Burney Basin country there's Cross in a Box and Sixty-Six. What about it?"

"How about Spoon?" asked Haslam. "You ever put any Spoon cattle in cars?"

"Spoon? Now who —" Foskett broke off, the wariness in him deepening, while a frown of worry pulled a deep furrow between his somewhat bulgy eyes. "Say, who you askin' for, anyhow? I don't remember ever seein' you before."

"I," said Haslam dryly, "arrived the other

night. Along with some others, I was met by a reception committee, headed by Hugh Racklyn. During the festivities, I threw a Rocking R bucko in your face. You must remember that?"

Nate Foskett slipped into definite retreat. "I took no sides in that fuss," he asserted hurriedly. "I never take sides. I just do my work and mind my own business."

"Fine!" applauded Haslam. Twisting up a cigarette, he kept eyeing Foskett steadily. "The smartest men I know do their work and mind their own business. But part of your business should be giving me a straight answer on what I asked you. Any Spoon cattle ever shipped out of here?"

A sudden glisten on Nate Foskett's face turned into a big blob of sweat which trickled down and lost itself under the curve of a whiskery jowl. Riley Haslam, observing, kept up his relentless probing.

"I'll put it another way. You ever ship any Spoon cattle, vented to either Rocking R or Two Link?"

Another blob of sweat ran down the agent's face. And Foskett knew for a certainty that it wouldn't do him a bit of good to try and bluff or side-step here. So he came through.

"Mebbe close on a hundred by Rocking

171

R, and between fifty and seventy-five by Two Link."

"Well mixed in among straight Rocking R and Two Link stuff, I suppose?"

"Could have been. What's wrong with that? When a man buys up any branded stuff, he always vents to his own iron, doesn't he? He's got that right, ain't he?"

"Why sure he has," soothed Haslam, "just so long as he did buy them. You checked up on that point, I suppose?"

Nate Foskett was really sweating now, and breathing heavily besides, causing him to wheeze a little. "Why should I check? None of my business. I tell you I don't ask questions and I don't take sides. I just —"

"I know," broke in Haslam. "You just mind your business and do your work. Diligent hombre, that's you. Stay with it and one of these days you may own the railroad."

Haslam turned and went out. Nate Foskett pushed his big stomach back into the kitchen and gulped greedily at a toddy that had gone slightly cold. By the time the glass was empty, he was feeling a little better, well enough to go into a flurry of cursing, directed at any and all who were curious. He hated questions and he hated people who asked them. For a man never knew. . . .

Cutting back across the open interval between the station and the town, Riley Haslam recalled another night when he'd made this crossing, and of the difference in his affairs then, and now. Beaten and sick and desperate, his fortunes that night had been about as low as he could ever remember. Then, when things were at their apparent worst, out of the dark had come that girl, Janet Wilkerson, and from the moment she extended a helping hand to him, things had mended steadily.

It was, he mused, as though her appearance marked a turning point in life for him. He knew that such things could happen. A man was supposed to be master of his own destiny, and to some extent perhaps he was. But there was always a percentage of unguessed influences at work, too, and a man never knew when one of these might touch him.

With him, the influence had been the generous impulse of a slip of a girl with clear and honest eyes. A score of times since that first night, Haslam had thought of her. And every time he did, a scourging dissatisfaction with his empty past and equally empty immediate future had ridden him hard. He saw now that this dissatisfaction had been one of the spurs driving him to his break with Overdeck, while also having considerable to do with his decision to accept Cash Fletcher's offer of the Deer Creek Meadows venture. On such an unforeseen turn of events could a man's destiny rest.

While still some distance from the street, Haslam heard the mutter of hoofs and caught the run of movement which marked the arrival of several riders. They went right along to the Staghorn, dismounted there and went into the bar. With some wariness, Haslam headed there himself.

In the Staghorn bar things had pretty well settled down for the evening. Several poker tables were in use, cigar smoke wreathed and curled and the bartender carried an occasional drink to this or that table. Only the two latest arrivals were at the bar, waiting for service, and Cash Fletcher, calling to be dealt out for a few hands, left one of the tables to join them. He caught Haslam's eye as Haslam stepped in from the night and gave him a beckoning nod.

"Meet Rufe Wilkerson and Walt Heighly," said Fletcher. "Rufe — Walt, shake hands with Riley Haslam. While he won't be exactly a next-door neighbor of yours, you'll probably be seeing him around considerable. For he's Scuffy Elrod's new partner, and he's opening up Scuffy's Deer Creek Meadows range again."

This was startling news to Rufe Wilkerson and Haslam saw that it was so. Wilkerson's handshake was brief, impersonal, and he studied Haslam with a quick searching. Walt Heighly was also startled, but there was a solid pressure in his hand-grip that gave Haslam to wonder.

Rufe Wilkerson turned to Cash Fletcher. "Is Elrod handling this himself, or are you acting for him?"

"I am," admitted Fletcher quietly, "along with Doc Jay and Len Pechard. You know it couldn't be otherwise, Rufe — with Scuffy in the shape he is. Doc and Len and me, we've taken care of other things for Scuffy, so we can see no good reason why we shouldn't handle this."

Wilkerson, bluntly stubborn and out-spoken, said, "It will stir up trouble, which you well know. It could have been handled otherwise."

"How?" Cash Fletcher met Wilkerson's bluntness with some of his own. To the bartender, who had just come up, Fletcher indicated the whole of the small group. "On the house, Pete." Then he looked at Wilkerson again and again asked, "How, Rufe?"

"You could have probably leased the range to Hugh Racklyn," said the cattleman. "You know how Hugh feels about those meadows."

"He feels," said Fletcher dryly, "just like Syl Overdeck does. I can't recall Racklyn or Overdeck making any offer to lease the meadows, ever. By every indication, all either of them wants is a chance to move into the meadows, to take them and keep them, and to hell with the right or wrong of it, and to hell with Scuffy Elrod's interests. Now Doc and Len and me, we just can't see Scuffy being cold-decked and shut out that way. So, we've got him a partner. I agree that Racklyn isn't going to like the idea, nor will Overdeck. But I'm afraid they'll just have to get used to it."

A flush of feeling had been steadily climbing in Rufe Wilkerson's blunt cheeks, and now some anger sharpened his tone.

"Implications there I don't like, Fletcher. You know damned well that Hugh Racklyn is my good friend and neighbor, and I don't take kindly to any talk against him. I'm not too sure I want to take this drink with you."

Walt Heighly stirred uneasily and looked away. Cash Fletcher tipped a weary hand. "All right, Rufe — all right. I want no quarrel with you. Consider everything unsaid except the word that Haslam is taking over."

Wilkerson hesitated, still edgy. Then he picked up his glass and tossed off the drink. But he wasn't done with this thing, so now he turned to Riley Haslam.

"And just what do you figure to get out of this deal?"

Haslam, meeting Wilkerson's demanding stare across the edge of his glass, downed his drink before answering.

"Doc Jay said it might be a violent death and a shallow grave. He could be right. It will be interesting to find out."

There was a vague mockery in Haslam's tone and words which Wilkerson did not miss. The cattleman's stare became a slightly wary measuring.

"You're not long in this country."

"Not long," admitted Haslam. "But long enough to already recognize a couple of debts I aim to collect. One from your good friend and neighbor, Mr. Racklyn. For a beating he and some of his bucko lads handed me the night I arrived here."

"Ah!" exclaimed Wilkerson. "So that's it, eh?"

"That's it. Your Rocking R friends did their best to cave my ribs in, stomp me to death. They might have made a job of it, too, but for the kindness of a few people. One in particular, a young lady who helped me find shelter. There's another debt I owe. She's got certain opinions, that young lady has. Maybe I can square my debt to her by proving her opinions right."

By now, Walt Heighly was staring at Haslam with a bright and not unfriendly interest, while Rufe Wilkerson, though the flush of anger still lay in his face, gave evidence of backing away from an issue that had become stickery.

"I don't know what you're talking about," he said gruffly.

"The hell you don't!" Haslam retorted. "You know exactly what I'm driving at. Now I'm asking you a question, seeing that you've asked me a couple. To your knowledge, Wilkerson, did Hugh Racklyn ever buy any cattle from Scuffy Elrod?"

Cash Fletcher spoke up quickly. "Maybe that sort of thing, Riley, had better —"

"No!" Haslam cut in, "no maybes, Cash. I've taken on a job. Now I'm going after some answers in my own way." He turned to Wilkerson again. "You got an answer for me, friend?"

"How would I know anything about that?" said Wilkerson acidly. "Hugh's business is his own. I don't stick my nose into my neighbor's affairs."

"Could be times when you should," said Haslam. "And maybe this is one of them. For if Racklyn never bought any cattle from Elrod, he sure as hell stole them. I understand he's shipped a good hundred head of Spoon stock, vented to his Rocking R stuff. I've seen them with my own eyes. So, either Racklyn bought 'em or he stole 'em. He better have a bill of sale to prove the first. For that he's going to have to show me!"

The metallic chirr of dragging spur chains and spinning rowels sounded at the Staghorn doorway, and Haslam glanced that way to see Bud Caddell, the kid rider of Two Link, come in. Pausing just inside the door, the young rider let his glance run around the room. He met Haslam's eyes, nodded, moved over to the far end of the bar and waited there. To Wilkerson, Heighly and Cash Fletcher, Haslam said, "Friend of mine, yonder. Wants to see me about something." He crossed over and dropped in beside Bud Caddell.

"Something stirring you, kid?"

Bud reddened, squirmed, answered awkwardly. "I ain't enjoying this a bit. I'm just following orders. I feel like a damned fool."

Haslam dropped a hand on the youngster's arm, smiling slightly. "Get rid of it. I won't mind."

"Well," said Bud lamely, "Syl Overdeck sent me to town to try and locate you and Frank Didion. It's about the broncs you and Didion rode, and the one you brought that wounded Rocking R hand in on. Overdeck says the broncs are his and he wants them back right away." Heaving a sigh of relief, the kid added, "That does it. I've told you. It's all I said I'd do, which was deliver the message. And I'm saying again, there sure ain't nothing personal about it. You believe that, don't you?" he ended anxiously.

Haslam's smile widened. "Sure. Sure I do, kid. I understand, and there's no hard feelings. But now I'm going to give you a message to take to Overdeck. You tell him to come himself to collect those broncs. And tell him to bring along the bill of sale covering the Spoon cattle he bought from Scuffy Elrod. When he shows me that bill of sale, he gets the horses back. But not until."

Bud blinked a couple of times, obviously puzzled. "Mebbe I'm thick-headed," he blurted. "But I don't see the connection. What's a bill of sale for some cattle bought from a guy named Elrod got to do with three Two Link broncs?"

"You haven't been with Two Link very long, have you, kid?" said Haslam. "Not long enough to know about some of these things. Well, I'll fill in a couple of angles for you. A fellow named Elrod owned Deer Creek Meadows. He still does. But some time back he ran into hard luck. He was dragged by his horse, so some claim, and he came out of it all broken up and unable to work his range any more. At the time he was hurt Elrod had maybe as many as three hundred head of cattle running under his brand, the Spoon. Well, the cattle have kinda disappeared. Me, I'm Elrod's new partner. I'm taking over Deer Creek Meadows, and I'm looking for Spoon cattle — that disappeared. Now you begin to understand?"

Bud Caddell understood, all right. Color burned in his lean young cheeks and his blue eyes flashed.

"I never did try and kid myself that Two Link was any sweetness-and-light outfit. I knew from the start that it was a pretty rough, tough layout. Which was all right with me — up to a point. That point is plumb reached and passed when there's any question about cattle packing the Two Link iron. I've seen that vented Spoon brand. Hell! I even helped drive some of them right here to the pens in Palisade for shipping. Now you're saying —"

"Nothing for dead certain, Bud," cut in Haslam. "I could be guessing. But all

Overdeck has to do to prove I'm guessing wrong is show that bill of sale. Buy you a drink to keep you warm on the ride home?"

Bud Caddell shook his head. "I got things to think about that'll keep me warm." He started to turn to the door, then hesitated over both the move and his question. "You say you're takin' over Deer Creek Meadows. Seeing the way Syl Overdeck's been feeling toward Rocking R moving in there, that means you and Overdeck could meet head on?"

"I reckon so, Bud — if Overdeck tries to push the question."

"Is Frank Didion going to ride with you?"

"Yeah, he is."

"Then I sure got things to think about," said the young rider soberly. "I — well — good luck!"

He hurried out and Haslam turned back along the bar. Rufe Wilkerson and Walt Heighly had left the bar and moved over to sit into one of the table games. Cash Fletcher, puffing a cigar and staring thoughtfully into the back bar mirror, spoke quietly without turning his head.

"What did that Two Link rider want?"

"Overdeck sent him in after those Two Link saddle broncs Frank Didion and I got feeding down in the livery corral. I told the kid to tell Overdeck to come after the broncs himself and to bring along a bill of sale covering the Spoon cattle now vented to Two Link. No bill of sale, no broncs."

"Hah!" murmured Fletcher. "Going to charge the worth of the horses against what Two Link owes on Spoon cows, that it?"

"That's it! And then collect every damn cent due besides. The same goes for Racklyn and the Rocking R. Maybe you wondered why I put it so straight and strong to Wilkerson about Rocking R. Well, as I see Wilkerson, while he's stubborn enough to be blindly loyal to a past friendship, he's fundamentally honest and a square shooter. And once he brings himself to admit a fact, that will be that. Starting now, he's going to be wondering and thinking about Spoon cattle like he never did before. He's going to be asking Racklyn questions about vented brands. And when Racklyn doesn't have any answers good enough to suit, Rufe Wilkerson is going to ride away from Racklyn."

"If that happens," said Fletcher, "it will hurt Racklyn badly. For every friend a man loses, he's weakened that much. Knowing Racklyn, it will probably make him ride wilder than ever."

"Which is what we want," Haslam said.

"We want him to start pushing his hand. You've played your share of poker, Cash. Tell me, who is the easiest to trim, over the long run?"

"The one who persists in forcing the bets, of course," admitted Fletcher. "He may overpower the game for a while, but sooner or later he gets caught in the big bind. So, play this your own way, Riley. I won't question it."

It was pushing close to midnight when Bud Caddell got back to Two Link headquarters. All lights were out, the place was asleep. Bud put up his horse, paused at the door of the bunkhouse to pull off his boots, then went on in to his bunk, moving noiselessly in his socks. He eased himself into the blankets, then lay there, staring with wide eyes into the blackness overhead, only vaguely conscious of the sleeping men around him.

For Bud Caddell was wrestling with a deeply personal problem. He had done a lot of serious thinking during the ride out from town, and the summation of that thinking had left him with a vast unease and restlessness. These feelings held him now, sleepless. Bud had a decision to make, providing certain things were so. And it could be a very important decision, one that could shape his whole future. It was, he realized, a choice that had to be all one way or all the other; there was no halfway point in the matter. Midnight was a full hour gone before he got to sleep.

He was the last up and to breakfast and by the time he'd finished and left the cookshack, Ben Spawn had already ordered the other Two Link riders about their day's work. For Bud Caddell, the foreman had a surly nod of direction toward the ranch house.

"Overdeck wants to see you in the office, Caddell. Get over there!"

This last was in Spawn's most aggressive growl and Bud, turning toward the ranch house, wondered at the sourness of a man who could not give an order without discoloring it with overbearing arrogance.

The room Syl Overdeck called his office was a corner one, holding a cluttered table, half a dozen chairs and a couple of shelves stacked with ranch records. Overdeck was sitting behind the table, smoking a black, twisted cheroot when Bud Caddell walked in. Syl Overdeck wasted no time coming to the point.

"You get a line on Haslam and Didion and those broncs of ours?"

Bud Caddell nodded slowly. "Yeah. I saw Haslam and talked to him. I gave him your message about the broncs."

"He turn 'em over to you?"

"No. He said if you wanted the broncs to come after them yourself. And that —"

Syl Overdeck slammed a fist on the table. "What's he stalling about? He trying to play horse thief? The animals are mine and he damn well knows it!" He turned his quick rising anger on the young rider. "Maybe you didn't argue him tough enough, Caddell."

"Wasn't my place to argue him tough," said Bud quietly. "All I was supposed to do was tell him what you said. I did that. Now I'm telling you what he said. Maybe I better get something else out of the way, first. Haslam said to tell you that, as Scuffy Elrod's partner, he's taking over Deer Creek Meadows, and that Frank Didion is riding with him."

The possibility of such a thing taking place was so remote in Syl Overdeck's mind that for a moment or two Bud Caddell's quiet words did not register. When they did, the reaction brought Overdeck off his chair with a startled lunge.

"Haslam — taking over Deer Creek Meadows? What the hell are you talking about, Caddell?"

At this moment the door opened and Ben Spawn came in. He had caught just the last of Overdeck's words and, as he laid his heavy glance on Caddell, he asked, "He givin' you any lip, Syl? He is, I'll smooth him out. He's been goin' a mite uppity on us lately."

Overdeck turned his narrow face on Spawn. "You get tough in the wrong places, Ben. Haslam was the hombre you should have worked on. Wish to God you'd left him wherever it was you first met him. I got news for you. Haslam's taking over Deer Creek Meadows as Scuffy Elrod's partner. Didion will be riding with him. Now what do you think of that?"

As it had with Overdeck, it took a couple of moments for the news to register with Ben Spawn. When it did, he charged furious words at Bud Caddell. "You're lyin'! If you brought that word out, you're lyin'! I got a notion to —"

Syl Overdeck's voice cut harshly over Spawn's. "Shut up, Ben!"

Now that Overdeck had recovered from the first jolt of surprise, his mind was rapidly weighing the pros and cons of the matter. Dropping back into his chair, he drew deeply on his cheroot, then scowled into the bloom of smoke he blew from his lips. He spoke as though voicing a thought aloud.

"Haslam never cooked up any partnership agreement with Elrod on his own. I see the fine hand of somebody else behind all this."

Ben Spawn, still eyeing Bud Caddell sulkily, blurted, "Whose fine hand, Syl?"

Overdeck did not answer him. Instead, he fixed his glance on Bud Caddell again and asked a question of his own. "Did Haslam give you any idea who was backing him?"

Bud shook his head. "I've told you everything he told me, except one more thing."

"What's that?"

"Has to do with those broncs. Like I told you, he said for you to come after them yourself. And when you did, to bring along the bill of sale coverin' the Spoon cattle you got vented to your brand."

For a second time, Syl Overdeck was jolted. A heavy flush swept across his face and his eyes pinched down. "Meaning what, by that crack?"

Bud Caddell shrugged and drew a deep breath, knowing that the decision he'd been searching for all last night was now right before him, and knowing also exactly what it had to be. The knowledge relaxed him, loosened him up, sent a poised coolness all through him. He met Overdeck's narrowed glance with grave steadiness.

"Meaning, I guess, just what he said. He's seen the Spoon brand vented to Two Link. So have I. Haslam wants to see that bill of sale covering transfer of those cattle. And — so do I."

"What the hell business is it of his, or yours, either?" snapped Overdeck. "Maybe Ben here is right — maybe you are getting a little bit too uppity, Caddell."

Bud Caddell kept right on looking at Overdeck and now he knew, without further words, that there wasn't any bill of sale, that there never had been. He turned abruptly to the door, paused there.

"You can make out my time, Mr. Overdeck," he said evenly. "I'm going over to pack my gear, now!"

Bud Caddell went out, closing the door firmly behind him. Syl Overdeck threw his cheroot butt aside, cursed bitterly. Out of the clutter on the table he located both time and check books. He did some figuring, wrote out a check and flipped it across the table to Ben Spawn.

"Damned young whelp!" he said thinly. "Thinks he's smart as hell, he does — and that he's too good to ride with us any more. Take that check out to him, Ben — and when you give it to him, you can add anything else you've a notion to."

Ben Spawn, eyes glinting with anticipation, took the check and went over to the corrals. Presently Bud Caddell, lugging his frugal gear, emerged from the bunkhouse, crossed to the corrals, where he shook out a rope and caught up a solid-looking chestnut bronc which was his own personal property. He saddled up, tied on his gear, then glanced over at the ranch house and started that way. Ben Spawn, who'd been leaning against the corral fence, watching proceedings, pushed clear of the fence as he spoke.

"Here's your time, Caddell."

Ben Spawn held out the check with his left hand and, as Bud Caddell reached for it, lashed out suddenly with a knotted, treacherous right fist. The blow was savage and unexpected. It caught the young rider solidly under the left eye and drove him staggering back, the half-received check fluttering from his fingers.

With a gusty breath of eagerness, Ben Spawn leaped to follow up his treacherously gained advantage. This he had been looking forward to. For he was remembering the faint, sardonic smile he'd surprised on Bud Caddell's lips several times since the night when, beaten and disheveled and dripping river water, he'd made it a foot journey all the way out from town, rather than try and get his line-backed dun horse from the livery corral, and so dare the chance of further manhandling by Hugh Racklyn and the Rocking R crowd.

And then, when Haslam had made him take water on who was to ride the dun, and later out at Deer Creek Meadows, Bud Caddell's sardonic amusement had shown even plainer, offending the warped vanity that lay behind Spawn's natural brutishness. So Spawn had been promising himself something like this and, now that the chance was here, he let go all stops.

Bud Caddell, half stupefied from Spawn's first blow, sensed Spawn's onrush and instinctively rolled head and shoulders away from it, and Spawn's reaching fist was barely short. But his charging bulk slammed into Caddell and pinned him against the corral fence. Holding Caddell there with a driving shoulder, Spawn pumped two wicked smashes to Caddell's lank midriff. The punishment brought the young rider over, gasping for breath. And then Spawn stepped back slightly and ripped both fists to Caddell's head. Bud Caddell went down.

He lay there, gagging for air, rolling his numbed head from side to side. Then, as the first impact of rage began striking through the daze and the stupefaction, he struggled upright, stumbled inside Spawn's swinging blow, drove a short, overhand punch to Spawn's mouth. It cut Spawn's lips, brought blood, and shook Spawn up for a moment. But, with renewed fury, Spawn came back to the attack.

The loose lankiness of boyhood was still in Bud Caddell, and while there was nothing lacking in the kid's spirit, he couldn't match the physical burliness of Ben Spawn. So he had to give way, backing along beside the corral fence, numbed and staggering, taking a savage whipping, managing only occasionally to land an ineffectual blow.

He went down again and huddled with sagging head, physical sickness shrinking his world down to a gray dullness of light and sound. Ben Spawn drove a boot into his side, cursing him, telling him to get up and take it again. When this evoked no response, Spawn swung his boot a second time, then turned and stamped away, mopping at his bleeding mouth.

Long minutes passed before Bud Caddell could haul himself to his feet, find his horse and make the even more difficult haul into his saddle. But he managed it finally, and then he rode away, weaving a little from side to side.

# CHAPTER VIII

Rufe Wilkerson's Running W headquarters stood on a benchland on the west side of Cold River, some eight miles north of town and a half mile above where Tempest Creek, after driving tumultuously from its canyon in the Chevrons, slowed its hustling pace somewhat before finding confluence with the river.

Almost due east beyond the river and hidden by a barrier of several timbered miles lay Hugh Racklyn's Rocking R, with its wide sweep of lava badlands range that held a thousand small grassy flats and hidden draws where cattle could feed and fatten. Beyond all this ran Hatchet Rim, an eternally grim presence, dark and frowning. South of Rocking R, and dividing it from Syl Overdeck's Two Link range, ran the Deer Creek Meadows, cutting almost straight from the river to the rim and to Big Saddle Pass.

As he stood by a corner of the corrals and squinted into morning's sunrise blaze slanting in from beyond the distant black line of the rim, this was the world in broad aspect as Rufe Wilkerson visualized it.

There was a gravity in him and a troubled thoughtfulness, product of a nagging internal conflict that would not let him rest; a conflict that had been jolted into life at his meeting with Riley Haslam last night in the Staghorn. Just now, Rufe Wilkerson was trying to figure out how far his hatred of one man could blunt and blind his conscience to the acts of another.

All the way home from town last night, Wilkerson had pondered that question. It had been chiming in his mind when he went finally to sleep, and it had been his first thought on awakening this morning. Now it was still biting and gouging at him.

Where had his dislike of Syl Overdeck first started? It had, no doubt, always been there in part, one of those instinctive animosities men sometimes know, a product of clashing personalities as wide apart as the poles. But there had been incidents, too, on which the dislike had grown and fattened. Like that deal, back some five years ago, when, against Overdeck's given word that they were top string, half a dozen cavvy mounts, bought from Two Link on an emergency need, turned out to be culls.

When called to account on it, Overdeck had shown a shrug and sarcastic smile while remarking that a horse trade was a horse trade.

Then there was the time when Running W had ordered in a dozen cars to take out a beef shipment. When the herd had been carefully gathered and driven to Palisade, he was to find that Overdeck had moved in ahead, bullied the flaccid Nate Foskett into letting him have the cars, so putting a Two Link shipment of cattle on the road to catch a price crest which the Running W herd missed.

There had been, from time to time, other minor irritations and always, when he'd put over a slick deal at the expense of someone else, there would be that gleam of calculated and mocking triumph in Overdeck's eyes. And these were the sort of things which had enlarged and toughened Rufe Wilkerson's first instinctive dislike of the man into what was now an open, flat hatred.

Because of that hatred it had been an entirely natural reaction on his part to side immediately and strong with his sympathies with Hugh Racklyn, when feud flared and broke openly between Racklyn and Overdeck. For Racklyn was his nearest neighbor, had done him a number of favors, and was both seeing and being seen with definite approval for and by his eldest daughter, Cora.

But now — what about Racklyn?

That fellow Haslam, last night in the Staghorn, had put it so damned bluntly. Either, so Haslam said, Hugh Racklyn had bought those Spoon cattle, or he'd stolen them. To prove the one thing, and disprove the other, he'd have to be able to show a bill of sale. And — could he?

Wilkerson stirred, jabbed with that mental spur. He'd seen some Spoon brands vented to Rocking R. He'd never questioned Racklyn about them, nor had Racklyn ever remarked about them in any way of his own accord. And a couple of times Wilkerson had wondered. For he remembered Scuffy Elrod's accident very well, the time and the circumstance. And now, as he recalled these things, he realized he'd seen none of those vented brands until after Elrod's mishap.

Wilkerson got out his tobacco, was building a smoke, when Walt Heighly came up beside him, and Wilkerson knew a quick sweep of warm feeling. Here was a good man, a mighty good man, sound, reliable, trustworthy. You never had to guess about Walt Heighly in any way. You knew.

Heighly spoke quietly. "Get it figured out, Rufe?"

Wilkerson's answer was gruff. "How'd you know I was trying to?"

The Running W foreman's grin was brief. "Know you better than you know yourself, at times. One thing you might as well realize and acknowledge now as later. Either a thing is, or it isn't. No halfway, Rufe."

"Meanin'?"

Walt Heighly shrugged. "My opinion. You probably wouldn't like it. I've had it for some time."

"You don't like Hugh Racklyn, do you?" asked Wilkerson bluntly.

Heighly reached over, lifted Wilkerson's sack of tobacco from the vest pocket where Wilkerson had tucked it, spun up a deft cigarette. Not until he lit the smoke and drew the first deep inhalation, did he answer. Then he met Wilkerson's eyes steadily.

"No, Rufe," he said. "No, I don't like him. I never have."

"You've covered your feeling pretty well," said Wilkerson with some sharpness.

Heighly shrugged again. "One man's opinion is just — one man's opinion. I could be wrong."

"Maybe," growled Wilkerson, "Cora might have something to do with how you feel?"

A small tide of color seeped across Walt Heighly's face, and a glint of anger shone in his steady eyes. "I think a lot of Cora. Maybe if you thought as much, you wouldn't be so God damned pigheaded and blind!"

Jolted by his foreman's flat statement, Wilkerson rumbled in stubborn anger, "Pigheaded and blind, eh? About what?"

Walt Heighly made a weary gesture. "You know, Rufe — you know. Why don't you admit it? That fellow Haslam was shooting just about dead center, last night. You don't want to believe it, but deep inside, you know he was hitting the truth."

"Even he left the door open," argued Wilkerson. "He wasn't sure there wasn't a bill of sale. For that matter, who the hell is he to question anything or anybody in these parts? Just a tramp gunfighter who's drifted in. Cash Fletcher's a fool to have anything to do with him."

"Maybe, maybe not," said Walt Heighly. "I never figured Cash Fletcher as anybody's fool, and from what I saw of this fellow Riley Haslam, anybody who sees him as just a run of the mill two-bit gunfighter is making a big mistake. Me, I kind of liked the cut of his jib."

Wilkerson took a final deep drag at his

cigarette, dropped the butt and ground it to shreds under a vehement boot heel, then bit out a harsh question.

"Walt, I want a straight answer to a straight question. Do you think Hugh Racklyn vented a brand he had no right to?"

The corner of Walt Heighly's mouth curled up in a mirthless smile. "Just can't bring yourself to saying the plain words, can you, Rufe? Well, I'll do it for you. Yes, I think Racklyn stole Spoon cattle and vented to his brand. I knew Scuffy Elrod pretty well. I knew that the feeling between him and Racklyn wasn't exactly friendly, for Racklyn had been pushing at him for some time over the right to move cows back and forth through Big Saddle Pass. And that was an idea that didn't set well with Scuffy at all."

Wilkerson tossed an impatient hand. "I know all about that. But that's no proof—"

"Maybe not," cut in Heighly. "But knowing how Scuffy felt toward Racklyn, I can hardly see him sellin' cows to Racklyn. And as I recall, it wasn't until after Scuffy was dragged that the vented brands began to appear. Not only as Rocking R, but as Two Link, too."

"Expect anything of that whelp Overdeck," said Wilkerson harshly. "But do you realize, Walt, what you're doing when you say what you have about Hugh Racklyn?"

"Hell — Rufe, of course I do!" said Heighly explosively. "I'm calling him a damn cow thief! Rufe, when are you going to wake up about that fellow? He's not good for you, or for Cora, or for anyone else. There's poison in him!"

Rufe Wilkerson, jolted as he hadn't been for a long, long time, stared bleakly at his foreman, then shot another harsh question.

"How long you been feeling this way, Walt? About Racklyn, I mean?"

"Just about from the time I first laid eyes on him, I guess."

"Why didn't you ever say anything?"

Walt Heighly shrugged. "Would you have thanked me? Don't believe you would. More likely you'd have given me my time. Besides, he hadn't really done you or yours any real harm yet, and I figured that given time, you'd see the true picture on your own. But now things are shaping up. This fellow Haslam is liable to push a lot of things into the open. When and if he does, I want to see Running W affairs standing clean and square and straight up and down. I just happen to feel that way about the outfit and the family who owns it."

The bleakness of Rufe Wilkerson's expression broke slightly and he dropped a hand on his foreman's arm. "You'll do, Walt — any old time," he said gruffly. His glance struck down along the river again, and he stiffened, for down there along the narrow flat a rider had swung into view. "Speak of Haslam," he exclaimed, "and he comes riding. That's him, ain't it? Now what would he be wanting out here?"

Walt Heighly had his look, then said, "Haslam, all right. Whatever he wants, you won't have to guess long, Rufe. That fellow talks straight from the shoulder."

Over at the ranch house a screen door slammed and Janet Wilkerson, dressed for riding, came into the morning's sunlight and strode with her quick, brisk grace over to her father and Walt Heighly. She eyed them shrewdly.

"What are you two so sober about?" she wanted to know. "You should be expanding all over on a perfect morning like this. Walt, would you presently catch up some horses for Cora and me? Town calls my big sister and I'm going along."

"Sure, Janet — sure," nodded Walt Heighly. "Just as soon as I see what that fellow yonder wants."

Janet followed Heighly's nod, caught her

breath slightly, a faint tint of color washing through her cheeks.

"Baby," said Rufe Wilkerson, "you go on back to the house and wait there. Scamper, now!"

"Baby" didn't scamper. She tucked a hand under her father's arm and stayed put. Before Wilkerson could order her further, Riley Haslam, astride the line-backed dun horse, came swiftly up the short slope from the river flat, surveying the Running W headquarters with a swinging glance, then crossed to Wilkerson and Walt Heighly and Janet. He tipped his head slightly and touched the brim of his hat.

"Morning. Looks like I'm on the wrong side of the river."

Wilkerson eyed him searchingly, studying this man in daylight to see if it would bring out more than the night had. Haslam was fresh-shaven, and with the stain of past bruises virtually gone, his features showed clean and sharp and hard.

"Depends on what you were looking for," Wilkerson said briefly. "If it's Rocking R you want, then you'll have to cross the river."

"Thanks," nodded Haslam. "I will do that when I leave here. But, seeing that I now have the chance, I'll ask you a question I didn't get around to, last night. You ever buy any cattle from Scuffy Elrod?"

Wilkerson shook his head. "I never did. You'll find no Spoon brands vented to Running W. Did you expect to?"

The ghost of a smile touched Riley Haslam's lips. "No, I didn't. I knew there had to be one honest cattleman in these parts."

"Then why ask me if I'd ever bought any Spoon cattle?"

"Just trying to find out if Elrod was in the habit of selling hereabouts instead of shipping. You see, Wilkerson, I expect to talk with some who won't be as open and straight with their answers as you."

"I know nothing about that," said Wilkerson stiffly, "and I don't want to."

The words seemed lost on Haslam, whose glance was now steadily on Janet Wilkerson. On her part, Janet met the glance and held it, though that soft touch of color still beat in her cheeks. For one great and breathless moment it seemed as though the two of them were alone and apart from all others, and in that moment both of them knew that the world would never be exactly the same again for either of them.

Riley Haslam's hand went again to his hat, and this time he took it off, and his voice ran low and deep.

"Just so you'll know I really meant it the

first time, Miss Wilkerson — thanks again!"

Rufe Wilkerson, being completely outside the aura of feeling that had touched these two, and knowing it, opened his mouth to speak with some anger. But it was Walt Heighly who spoke first.

"Friend, if you were aiming to cross the river so you could talk to Hugh Racklyn — now you won't have to. For, yonder he comes!"

There were more riders on the river flat, four of them, cutting across at an angle that would bring them up the slope to these headquarters. Wilkerson exclaimed softly, turning swiftly on Haslam:

"You'll lift no hand in violence on my land!"

Haslam, again the remote and cold and watchful stranger, gave a bleak, brief nod. "I will not make the first move."

Wilkerson, turning to watch the approach of Racklyn and his men, spoke with blunt authority.

"Baby, you get over to the house, I mean it!"

This time Janet obeyed, while Walt Heighly, unarmed, drifted away beside the corrals, crossed to the bunkhouse and slipped inside. Only a moment or two later he reappeared, sauntering. But now there was a gun belted on him, and another Running W hand, Mitch Connerly, appeared from nowhere to lounge with apparent idle unconcern in the bunkhouse doorway. Mitch's main interest in life seemed to be the careful manufacture of a cigarette, but leaning against the wall of the bunkhouse, just inside the door and quick to Mitch's hand, was a rifle.

Ten yards short of Wilkerson and Riley Haslam, Walt Heighly dropped an arm across the top rail of the corral and stopped there, relaxed but watchful. Haslam, missing none of this maneuvering, put a questioning glance on Heighly, which the Running W foreman answered with a faint but reassuring nod.

Coming steadily on at the head of his riders, Hugh Racklyn set his horse up with a heavy hand, started to speak to Wilkerson and then, as though warned by some quickening instinct, swiveled his full attention on Riley Haslam, his stare arrogant and measuring.

Haslam met it fully, thinking that here at last he was face to face with this man who had been steadily looming larger and larger across the trail. Until now, Riley Haslam's measure of Hugh Racklyn had been a fragmentary and confused thing, just a recollection of that first night when Racklyn had been one of several, beating and smashing at him; a powerful, brutal force, secure of triumph because of the advantage of surprise and the backing of numbers. But now, though he had three behind him, Hugh Racklyn, as Riley Haslam saw him, was alone, and so he had his good and full look at the man, and he let the solid weight of his feeling go with the look.

He marked the size and physical power of the man, judged Racklyn's face, with its bold and predatory jut of nose and jaw, and its strong coloring. These were features that could have been good, but in this case the good was drained away by a cold and cruel craftiness lying far back in the eyes, and by the betraying lines about the mouth, telling of a wildness that could break past all human discipline.

It was Racklyn who spoke first, and he drove a thin question at Rufe Wilkerson, while never taking his eyes off Riley Haslam.

"Who is this, Rufe? Where'd he come from?"

Haslam answered for himself. "I think you're guessing close, Racklyn. The name is Haslam!"

Racklyn rolled a little forward in his saddle, hands crossed and pressing on the horn. Again he threw his question at Rufe Wilkerson.

"What's he doing here, Rufe? Don't you know he's an Overdeck man? Bought and paid for by Overdeck, guns and all?"

"Was," corrected Haslam. "No longer, Racklyn. And I got news for you. Right now I'm partners with Scuffy Elrod and I'm scouting for Spoon cattle. You should be able to tell me something, there. For I've seen Spoon brands vented to your iron. And they tell me you've shipped right on a hundred head of such. That's so, isn't it, Racklyn?"

Listening to Haslam, watching him closely, a veiled guardedness settled over Hugh Racklyn.

"You're fooling nobody, mister," he said heavily. "How could you be any partner of Elrod's?"

"Suppose you ask Cash Fletcher or Doc Jay or Len Pechard about that," drawled Haslam. "But to get back to the cattle angle. How about it? You ever ship any of that vented stuff?" Haslam's tone was casual, but his glance was boring and demanding.

One of Racklyn's riders spoke up. "Just say the word, Hugh — and we'll finish the job on this smart hombre. This time we'll run him plumb out of the country. This time he won't dodge out on us."

Over by the corral fence, Walt Heighly cleared his throat vigorously. "Wrong time and place to talk so big and rough and tough, Hoag. You're fooling me not at all. If you were alone, your tail would be between your legs!"

Now Rufe Wilkerson spoke. "Keep out of this, Walt. No bite of yours."

"I'm making it so, Rufe," came back Heighly. "Me, I'm plumb tired of big noise, big wind, big strut. Time's come, Rufe, to either saddle up or walk. It's black, or it's white — and I want to know. Now Haslam yonder just asked a fair question and I'd like to hear a fair answer. How about it, Racklyn — you got a bill of sale to back up those vented brands?"

"Walt!" yelled Wilkerson. "Will you shut up?"

"No!" retorted Heighly. "It's black or it's white, Rufe. And I got to know."

Missing none of this, Riley Haslam eyed Walt Heighly with distinct approval. This was working out better than he could have hoped for. For where Racklyn might have bluffed and ignored any questioning by him, he couldn't afford to ignore the Running W foreman. For Rufe Wilkerson was watching and listening.

Anger burned in Hugh Racklyn. It swelled the cords of his throat, deepened the color in his cheeks to an almost choleric intensity, coated his eyes with a hot shining. There was a thickness in his words as he spoke to Wilkerson.

"Rufe, I don't like this. I ride in here as a friend. I find you cheek by jowl with a bought-and-paid-for gunfighter brought on to this range with Syl Overdeck's money. This gunfighter starts making some wild talk and your foreman backs his hand. No, I don't get it and I don't like it!"

Consciously or otherwise, Racklyn had wielded the lash in these words and Rufe Wilkerson's blunt features squared and lifted. "Maybe," he said sharply, "there's some things I don't like, either, Hugh. Maybe I don't like the way you keep side-stepping a straight question. Haslam's asked it, Walt's asked it. Now I'm asking it. How about those vented brands?"

"All right," shot back the badgered Racklyn, "how about them? What in hell's wrong with a vented brand?"

"Not a thing, Hugh — providing it's backed by a bill of sale to make it legitimate. You got a bill of sale, Hugh?"

The anger in Racklyn deepened into rage. The lines about his mouth cut deep and

209

cruel and wild. In that moment he became a man Rufe Wilkerson had never seen before, strange and distant.

"Whether I have or whether I haven't is none of your damn business, Rufe. Keep your nose out of things that don't concern you. Tell that mouthy foreman of yours to watch his talk before it gets him into more trouble than he can handle." Racklyn swung his head and stared at Riley Haslam with a sort of blank deadliness. "You should have kept on running when you had the chance, mister. Now — you're the same as dead!"

With these words, Hugh Racklyn swung his horse, set the spurs and surged away, his three riders bunched and pressing close behind him. They went back the way they had come, crossing the river, disappearing into the timber beyond.

Rufe Wilkerson watched them go, wordless, a certain weariness in the cast of his head and shoulders. Then he turned to face Riley Haslam, who met the look and spoke with a quiet gravity.

"If because of me you've lost something you valued, I'm sorry, Wilkerson."

Wilkerson shook his head. "If I've lost anything, it wasn't of value. I can see that clearly, now. I should have seen it long ago.

Maybe I did, and just wouldn't admit it to myself. The man's a thief, a God-damned common cow thief. There is no bill of sale to cover those Spoon cattle. There never was. He and Syl Overdeck — two of a kind. Just common cow thieves!"

Walt Heighly, twisting up a smoke, moved in closer. "If you were looking for some answers, Haslam — you got 'em. What now?"

Haslam, reaching for his own tobacco, stared out to the east, eyes narrowed. "At the time Scuffy Elrod got hurt he had something like three hundred head of stock packing his Spoon brand. Where'd they go? None on Elrod's Deer Creek Meadows range. Frank Didion and me, we checked that pretty close. May have been some drifted over Big Saddle Pass. Didion and me, we'll have a look over that way. We find any, fine and dandy. The rest, Hugh Racklyn and Syl Overdeck are going to have to make good on — in cash or critters."

"You may find it a pretty rough chore to collect," said Heighly.

"Probably," agreed Haslam dryly. "But the rougher the chore, the rougher the method."

Wilkerson spoke with some somberness. "Were I in your boots, Haslam, I'd pay considerable accord to Racklyn's final words. He'll do his best to make good on them. He can't afford not to, now."

"I've been killed by words before," Haslam said. "But so far they've always turned out to be a poor substitute for the real thing."

Rufe Wilkerson shrugged as he turned away toward the ranch house. "Your ride. Wish you luck."

Walt Heighly stared after his boss. "Rufe's feeling a little low right now. He made the mistake of hating Syl Overdeck so much he was blind to the real Hugh Racklyn. A man can get twisted up that way, you know. Gave him a jolt to see Racklyn as he really is."

"I'm wondering," murmured Haslam, "why you stood ready to back my hand?"

"I wouldn't try and fool you," said the Running W foreman bluntly. "It wasn't that I was so much for you as it was how much I was against Hugh Racklyn."

Riley Haslam smiled crookedly. "Nothing I like better than a man who speaks with a straight tongue. Anyway, I'm obliged."

He twisted in his saddle, threw another look at the ranch house, then pulled the dun around and dropped down the slope toward the river, heading south.

In the Running W ranch house, Rufe Wilkerson faced his two daughters gravely. To Janet he said, "You're not the sort, Baby, to say 'I told you so.' But in this case you've a right to. For that fellow is no damned good!"

A little tightly, Cora asked, "Who are you talking about, Father?"

"You know. Hugh Racklyn. You'll not see him again. He's no damned good!" ended Wilkerson repetitiously.

"And whose word are you taking for that?" Repression put a shrillness in Cora's voice.

Wilkerson shook his head wearily. "I didn't have to take anybody's word. I just used my eyes and my ears and my common sense — finally. A couple of times in the past I've wondered about the Spoon cattle I've seen vented to Rocking R. I never asked Racklyn about them until today. There's only two ways Racklyn could have got possession of the cattle. Either he bought them, or he stole them. If he bought them, he'd have a bill of sale — and not be afraid to show it. But he hasn't got a bill of sale. The man's a common cow thief. You hear me, Cora — you'll not see him again!"

Wilkerson went on through to the room he used for an office. Left alone, for a time there was a deep and moveless silence between the two girls. Janet was grave, big-eyed, watching her elder sister, who stood by a window, staring out at nothing, while she twisted and retwisted a pair of gauntlet riding gloves.

It was Cora who finally broke the silence, her voice now small and far away.

"Dad could be wrong, couldn't he, Baby?"

Janet crossed over, put her arms about her sister. She said nothing, and that was her answer.

# CHAPTER IX

With the warmth of midafternoon's sun striking between their shoulders, Riley Haslam and Frank Didion rode up into the black maw of Big Saddle Pass. Here the lava pushed in close on either hand, bleak and hostile, a world of black and broken rock which trapped the warmth of the day and built it up to a heat that started a roll of sweat at the edges of saddle blankets.

Here only a few fragments of the hardiest and most persistent brush found precarious rooting and the visible world seemed peculiarly lifeless. Even the sound of hoofs, ringing off the solid rock underfoot, was compressed to a swift nothingness. Frank Didion, riding ahead, pulled his horse up for a blow and let Riley Haslam move in beside him.

"This," observed Didion wryly, "might have been Big Saddle Pass to the man who first named it so, but had I been in his boots I'd have put a different brand on it. I'd have called it Gates of Hell, or some such. This is the deadest stretch I ever saw."

It led, some half hour later, into a fair, far country of what seemed at first to be endless timberland. But they found, on working into this, a world of open glades and grassy parks beyond this and that fringe of timber. It was, thought Haslam, as they rode deeper and deeper into it, as fine a timber range as he'd ever seen. Here and there lay water, trapped between low ridges or in a swing of meadow cupped by the timber. Some of these water holes were mere ponds which a man might toss a pebble across; others were small lakes, spreading anywhere from one to several acres in extent.

Just at sundown, Haslam and Frank Didion came out on the aspen-fringed edge of one of these, sending a wisp of plover to winging and crying along the shore, while further out a pair of wild mallards pitched swiftly up in a flurry of beating wings, and as they climbed into the last rays of the sun, metallic green fire struck and flashed from the drake's head and neck.

"Pretty," said Frank Didion. "Pretty as all hell."

They off-saddled here, built their fire and cooked coffee and bacon from the meager pack Didion had tied behind his saddle cantle. They watched dusk settle in, blue and still and then full dark came down and their whole world was the circle of light and warmth thrown by their fire. Somewhere in the outer dark their horses fed along the lake shore and presently there was the "hush-hush" of invisible wings and then two soft splashes well off shore. Frank Didion grinned into the flames.

"That old green-head drake and his betsy just come back home. Probably spend a kind of restless night, wonderin' about us."

They squatted on their heels and smoked their cigarettes and stared into the fire and let their thoughts run. Presently Didion stirred.

"I can kind of understand Overdeck and Racklyn rowing over Big Saddle Pass, Riley. What with it leadin' into country like this. Summer graze for a lot of cattle up here. Never saw better, of its kind."

Haslam nodded and said softly, "With no sign of Spoon cattle in it anywhere. There may be a few up here, but there can't be many, or we'd have picked up sign. Which means we got a sizable settlement coming from both Two Link and Rocking R. I had to have a look up here before tackling Overdeck and Racklyn. Now I know."

They built up the fire, slept with their feet to it and awoke to a still and shivering dawn.

The breath of the lake was a cold and writhing mist, thick enough to hide the far shore. They stirred up the fire, cooked and drank scalding coffee, caught and saddled and headed back for Big Saddle Pass. Day's warmth was building by the time they moved down through the pass into Deer Creek Meadows. When they hit the middle meadow and came in sight of the cabin, Haslam pulled up short. A saddled horse stood ground reined beside the cabin.

"Company, Frank."

Didion stared, then said, "I've seen that chestnut bronc with the white points before." Then, as a lanky figure moved from the cabin door, Didion murmured, "Ah! Of course. That's the kid, Bud Caddell. The chestnut is his own pet bronc. Out at Two Link he was always foolin' with it in his spare time. Now, what would bring him over here?"

They rode on in and Bud Caddell, noting their approach, moved out a little to meet them. Haslam, reining up, eyed the kid with some surprise, marking the signs of conflict.

"What is it, kid? What happened to you?"

"Ben Spawn. He gave me a going over."

"Why?"

Bud Caddell told them the story. "Doc Jay worked on me some and loaned me a bunk for the night," he ended. "When I told him I was lookin' for you, he said I'd probably find you out here. So — I rode out."

"What did you want to see me for, Bud?" Haslam asked.

The lanky youngster scuffed a boot toe in the dirt, then met Haslam's eyes steadily. "Want to ride with you and Didion. I'm all done out at Two Link. Syl Overdeck is a damn cow thief, and I want no part of him any more. Ben Spawn's of the same stripe."

Haslam spun up a cigarette and as he licked it into shape, he asked, "What makes you so sure about Overdeck being that way?"

"I braced him about those Spoon cows he's vented to Two Link. He just had no good answer at all, but side-stepped and dodged all over the pasture. Then he turned Ben Spawn loose on me, when I asked for my time."

"You figure to get back at those two by riding with Frank and me?" asked Haslam. "That why you're here?"

"Some," admitted the kid quietly. "Yeah, that's some of it. Not all, though. I got to ride somewhere and — well, I'd just like to ride with you, that's all."

Haslam studied the kid gravely, liking him as he had from the first. "I wouldn't bet on there being much of a future in it. Frank and me, we're due to be open game to Two Link and Rocking R. Which don't concern us too much, because we're old hands at that sort of thing and able to hand back as good as comes our way. But you've never mixed in that sort of thing and it's a good idea to stay away from. You'd be showing a lot better judgment, kid, if you went and saw Rufe Wilkerson and tried for a job with him. The Running W is a good, square outfit."

Bud Caddell gave Haslam back his steady survey. "Spoon aims to be a decent outfit, don't it? You're not aimin' to steal any cows or that sort of thing?"

"We're going to take every vented Spoon brand we can locate, unless somebody has a bill of sale to prove ownership."

"That," nodded the kid, "ain't stealin'. That's just getting back what's your own. I want to help. I don't want to ride for Rufe Wilkerson. I want to ride with you."

The kid was determined. His jaw was set, and behind bruise-puffed lids, his eyes were cool and steady.

"All right," decided Haslam abruptly. "It's a go. I'll probably work the devil out of you."

"I'll hold up my end there, too," vowed Bud stoutly.

★ ★ ★

They rode south through the broken lava, with the rim lunging up dark and brooding on their left. When they came in at the north end of the long-winding run of the Two Link pasture land, they paused in the shadow of a mahogany clump and took careful visual measure of what lay ahead.

Out there, some five or six hundred yards distant, half a dozen men were working cattle. Off to one side, two of these riders were holding a small bunch of white faces. The other four were spurring here and there among other scattered critters in an apparently aimless manner. That there was purpose here, however, showed a moment later when two of these roving riders closed in on a critter and hazed it along and put it in with the small held bunch.

Frank Didion stirred in his saddle and spoke softly. "What you think, Riley?"

"Could mean nothing, or it could mean a lot," answered Haslam. "But I am playing with the same thought you are."

Didion nodded. "Right now I can think of only two reasons why Overdeck would be parting out cattle like that. One would be if he was working up a shipping herd, which I doubt plenty, as it's too early in the season for that. The other would be if those critters being bunched carried maybe vented brands which Mr. Overdeck would like to get out of sight. I suggest we sit and watch awhile."

Haslam smiled thinly. "Let's."

They did, twisting up smokes, slouching at ease in their saddles. The air was warm, the shade of the mahogany clump welcome. A covey of mountain quail quirked complainingly as they moved off through the brush in a series of small flutterings. Faintly up from the stirring cattle came a protesting bellow.

Bud Caddell, restless, said, "Say they are vented brands. How we goin' to know and what are we goin' to do?"

"For the first, we'll take a look and for the second we'll take the critters," Haslam said.

"Six of them, three of us," said Bud.

Haslam's tone sharpened a trifle. "Warned you it could be rough, riding with Frank and me, didn't I?"

The young rider flushed under his bruises. "I was just wonderin'," he blurted. "Not tryin' to beg off or anything like that."

"Sure," said Haslam, milder again. "I know, kid."

"They're startin' to move out with that gather," warned Frank Didion. "If we're goin' to do anything about it, it better be now."

The gather was being headed south. Haslam considered a moment, then said, "We'll swing toward the river, hit the town trail, then cut back toward Two Link headquarters. We ought to meet up with them about there. And when I brace Overdeck about a bill of sale, he'll be close enough to the ranch house to go get it — if he's got such."

"He hasn't," said Didion. "But it should be interesting to hear what he has to say."

They rode their circle, back toward the river and south along it, and when they hit the town trail they cut into it and rode it swiftly back toward the rim and Two Link headquarters. And out there in the long north and south flat they met up with the driven gather.

There was a considerable stir of confusion among the Two Link contingent, and then, while four of the riders held the gather to a stop, it was Syl Overdeck and Ben Spawn who came on a little way, riding warily.

Haslam said, "We find out," and moved to meet them.

Syl Overdeck's thin, dark face was expressionless, but there was a glint in his black eyes telling of a taut alertness. Ben Spawn was his usual heavy, glowering self. Overdeck spoke curtly.

"You're on my land, Haslam — and not welcome!"

Haslam's smile was faintly sardonic. "Didn't figure to be. But I just had to know."

"Know — what?"

"What kind of brands that gather is packing. Whether any of them are vented. Now that I'm here, I'll have a look."

"Like hell!" Overdeck snapped. "You're getting off my land and staying off. Also, those broncs you and Didion are riding are mine, and I want —"

Overdeck broke off abruptly on a thin, breathy note. For of a sudden there was a gun in Haslam's fist and the muzzle of it was steadily in line with Overdeck's belt buckle. Just as suddenly, Haslam's faint smile was gone and his eyes and face and words were stony cold.

"Couple of things you'd better understand, Overdeck — once and for all. First, I didn't take over Deer Creek Meadows just to be long-winded out of any part of them, or out of one head of Spoon cattle that should be grazing those meadows. Second, I'm not going to play patty-cake with you or Racklyn or anybody else; I'm going to get results, the shortest and quickest way. Third, I'm not going to belly up big and stupid against out-sized odds and play the noble fool. So, here I got a gun on you and if any of your crowd start anything, you won't be around to see the finish. Now let's go have a look at those brands!"

The glint in Overdeck's eyes became a shifty flicker which moved away from Haslam long enough to touch Frank Didion and Bud Caddell and even Ben Spawn, before coming back to Haslam. Frank Didion, thoroughly still, was watching Ben Spawn, who knew it, and so held his own surly stillness.

Haslam pushed the dun ahead, crowding Overdeck's mount. "We go look at those brands," he said again.

Overdeck's words seemed strangled in his throat. "Damn you, Haslam — damn you —"

But he spun his mount and rode back to the gather, Haslam keeping even with him on the off side and almost stirrup to stirrup, and all the time that drawn gun lay across the saddle in front of him, holding Overdeck steadily under its threat.

The four riders with the gather made as if to fan out. "Hold them together, Overdeck!" ordered Haslam harshly. "Remember, it's your hide!"

Overdeck yelled an order and the four, uncertain and sullen, quieted down. Over his shoulder, Haslam said, "Kid, you look

225

through the gather. Read the iron on every critter in it. Then let me know."

Bud Caddell moved in, working his way around and through the restless, shifting cattle. Presently he came back. "All Spoon vented to Two Link," he reported.

"Ah!" said Haslam. "If you bought these cattle from Scuffy Elrod, then you'll have a bill of sale, Overdeck. I want to see it."

"I don't carry all my ranch records with me all the time," said Overdeck. "And for that matter —"

"If you haven't got it with you, where is it?" cut in Haslam.

"None of your damned business!" shrilled the badgered ranch owner. "I don't have to answer to you for anything, Haslam. You've got no authority to push me around, question me. You —"

Haslam waggled his gun slightly. "Authority enough for me, Overdeck. Now we quit stalling. You got no bill of sale. You, like Racklyn, are just another cheap rustler of the lowest kind. Stealing from a man unable to help himself, Scuffy Elrod. So now, in Elrod's name, I'm taking these cattle back to Deer Creek Meadows, where they belong. And you're riding along with Didion and the kid and me, just to make damn sure we get there. Tell your crowd off,

Overdeck. Send them back to headquarters."

Watching Overdeck narrowly, Riley Haslam saw the venom in the man swell and reek, congest his eyes and face, but back away from the dread certainty that lay in that free and waiting gun. Seeing this, Haslam nodded and said quietly, "Smart, Overdeck. You got me read exactly right. There's nothing noble in a game like this, so I never try and play it that way."

Overdeck waved a commanding arm, gave his order, and when his men hesitated uncertainly, gave it again in a furious rising yell. This moved them and they started off, only Ben Spawn lingering a moment.

"Somewhere," he said thickly, "this thing will change!"

"Anywhere, Ben," Frank Didion told him. "Anywhere and any time — if that's the way you want it!"

Spawn seemed not to hear, fixing his hot stare on Bud Caddell. "You," he said, "you moved into the wrong camp, as you'll find out!"

"Ben," drawled Didion, "you talk a ton. But I still think you run light weight. Git!"

Spawn held on a moment longer, having his final look at all of them. Then he whirled his horse, spurred it savagely and charged away.

Free of containing pressure, the gather of cattle began to spread and break, and Frank Didion and Bud Caddell were immediately busy, spurring back and forth, swinging rope ends. To Syl Overdeck, Haslam said, "You helped drive them away from Deer Creek Meadows, so now you can help drive them back. Get busy!"

There was nothing else Overdeck could do but obey. They brought the gather under control and moved it north and into the lavas. Didion and Bud Caddell contained the flanks, Haslam and Overdeck rode the drag.

Haslam had long since put his gun away, which Overdeck knew but also realized wisely enough that it made no difference now. All he could do was see this thing through as far as the Deer Creek Meadows, if Haslam forced him to ride that far. His turn, thought Overdeck, would come later, when he'd had his chance to plan a few moves. So the Two Link owner rode in silence, moved cattle along on his side of the drag, and contained all thought and feeling behind the dark mask of his face.

They came to the meadows and watched the cattle stream down into them. Haslam, sagging his weight into the stirrup, spun up a smoke.

"Look pretty, don't they, Overdeck?" he drawled. "Spoon cattle on Spoon range again. But these are only a small part of what should be there. Don't doubt but what there's some more scattered across your range. I expect to get them back, of course. Then there's the little matter of them you've already shipped. We'll accept a cash settlement for them. I'm going to be doing some careful adding and subtracting and when I come around to collect I don't expect to wait for the money. One more word. Starting now, Deer Creek Meadows and Big Saddle Pass are closed range to you and any of your riders. So — stay away!"

Haslam straightened in his saddle and headed down into the meadows, blue cigarette smoke curling past his face. Frank Didion and Bud Caddell followed him down. Left alone, Syl Overdeck stared after them, the thin darkness of his face beginning to twist and pull under the surge of emotions seething within him. He reined his horse hard around, heading back into the lavas, and now at last the stifling fury in him broke free, and he went through a frenzy of bitter cursing that left him drawn and sweating.

It left him also strangely quieted, and in the relief of this the idea came to him. He mulled it over as he rode along and its possibilities kindled a new gleam in his eye and put a hint of color in his swarthy cheeks. By the time he reached Two Link headquarters he had a lot of angles planned.

The Rocking R headquarters, being that of a bachelor outfit, had been built with an economy of creature comforts and little idea of attractiveness. The buildings were raw-boarded, squat and square. The four-room cabin which Hugh Racklyn was pleased to call his ranch house was no better than the rest, though it did have a narrow porch across the front of it.

Racklyn sat on that porch now, slouched deep in a chair, spurred heels hooked on the low rail of the porch. His mood was dark and the dead cigar stub in his mouth was chewed to tatters. He threw this aside as a rider broke from the timber at the southern end of the headquarters park and came on in at a wary jog. Idly watching the rider, Racklyn abruptly realized that this was not one of his Rocking R hands. He came upright in his chair and sent a reaching growl across the open toward the bunkhouse.

"Hey, Pres! Watch it!"

The lank, round-headed figure of Pres Hoag showed at the bunkhouse door, his stare following the direction of Racklyn's stabbing thumb. Hoag turned his head, spoke over his shoulder to someone in the bunkhouse, then propped a shoulder against the side of the doorway and waited there, narrowly watchful.

The rider came steadily on, swinging in past a point of the corrals and over to where Racklyn sat. Reining in, the rider put his mount broadside to Racklyn, who read the animal's brand clearly. Two Link.

Racklyn got to his feet, his glance boring at the rider. "You better have a damn good reason for showing here," he said. "What is it?"

The rider jerked his head across his shoulder. "Back there — in the timber. Syl Overdeck. He wants to have a talk with you. Sent me ahead to see if you'd give your word that he could ride in and ride out again without trouble."

Racklyn blinked his surprise. "Syl Overdeck — wants a talk with me?" he blurted. "What the hell about?"

The rider shrugged. "Got no idea. All I know is he wants to talk with you and wants your promise that he can come and go peaceful. How about it — yes or no?"

Racklyn considered, scowling. Here was a turn of events he hadn't dreamed of — that the time would ever come when he and Syl

Overdeck might get together for a peaceful talk. Suspicion was a pushing urgency inside him. A man would be all fool to trust such as Syl Overdeck. Still, under the conditions there was nothing Overdeck could do. And it never hurt to listen. . . .

Racklyn jerked a short nod. "Good enough. Tell him he can ride in and ride out, providing he behaves himself."

"He'd be a damn fool to try anything on your front porch, wouldn't he?" retorted the rider, heading away.

When the rider was out of earshot, Racklyn called over to Hoag again. "This will surprise you. Syl Overdeck's out yonder in the timber. He's coming in for a talk. He's not to be bothered, long as there are no tricks. But — spread a couple of the boys around, just in case."

Racklyn stepped into the ranch house, came out with another chair and a fresh cigar. Then he settled down to watch Syl Overdeck emerge from the timber and ride steadily up. Overdeck reined in and for several long moments these two men, bitter and unrelenting enemies, measured each other. It was Racklyn who spoke first.

"You wouldn't be here without some good reason. Maybe you'll talk easier if you're out of the saddle." He indicated the vacant chair.

Syl Overdeck hesitated, his glance swinging warily over the layout. Racklyn grunted caustically.

"Sure I got some of the boys watching you. What the hell did you expect? But behave yourself and you ride out as you came. Now — what's spurring you?"

Syl Overdeck stepped from the saddle, moved over to the waiting chair. He sat hunched forward a little, spinning up a smoke, his glance fixed on his busy fingers. He spoke slowly.

"Did it ever come to you, Racklyn, that you and me ain't been exactly smart over the past year or two?"

Racklyn considered him narrowly. "That could be a matter of opinion, either way. Go on!"

"We've been doing our damnedest to cut each other's throat," Overdeck said. "I can't see where it's gained either of us a thing. Now if we go on this way, eating each other up, somebody else is going to move in to grab off what you and me been rowing over. In fact, they've already moved in."

Racklyn took a deep drag at his cigar, let an uprunning veil of smoke winnow from his lips. "You're meaning Haslam, of course?"

"Meaning Haslam," nodded Overdeck.

"He's in Deer Creek Meadows. The talk is that he's there as Elrod's partner. That means he's got the weight of town opinion behind him, and, whether we like it or not, that counts, plenty! In his own right, Haslam's one damn tough hombre. He's got Frank Didion riding with him, now, and Bud Caddell, that kid I used to have in my outfit. The kid don't amount to much, but Didion does. He's an old hand at the rough game, just as Haslam is. Given a little time, they'll be set so deep in the meadows that neither you or me alone will be able to dig them out. Time is on their side. If we're going to do something, we better be about it."

Racklyn squinted into the distance with narrowed eyes. "What you're suggesting is that we throw in together, is that it, Overdeck?"

"That's it."

"That's almost funny, considering how we've been working on each other in the past." There was broad sarcasm in Racklyn's words.

"Funny or not, it still makes sense," argued Overdeck. "I'm being realistic about this. Sure, I'd like to have that summer range out past Big Saddle Pass all to myself. But by the same token, I'd rather have half of it than none at all. And none at all is what it will be with Haslam set in the meadows. That goes for you as well as for me. I'm saying we'd be smart to bury the hatchet, figure on a fifty-fifty split on that high summer range, and go after Haslam together."

"Boiled down," growled Racklyn, "what you're really after is to get me to pull the chestnuts out of the fire for you. You're afraid to go after Haslam. You want me to do it for you. Overdeck, I'm not that big a fool."

Overdeck, taking a final pull at his cigarette, flipped the butt past the porch rail, got to his feet. "You're seeing it in a pretty narrow way, Racklyn. Sure I'm afraid of Haslam. I'd be a fool if I wasn't. There's a streak of danger in that man as black and deep as hell. On top of that, whether you like it or not, he's honest. He is not, like you and me, a damned cow thief. And —"

Hugh Racklyn hit his feet, grabbed Overdeck by the arm, spun him around. The wildness was flaring in Racklyn's eyes. "That kind of talk I take from nobody," he growled thickly. "I gave my word that you could come and go without harm, Overdeck. But there are limits!"

Overdeck held Racklyn's furious gaze

steadily. "I learned a trick from you, Hugh, sometime back, after Scuffy Elrod was hurt and there was nobody to look after Spoon cattle. You began venting to Rocking R. So I took what I could find of them and vented to my iron. It all looked fine and fair on the surface. But it wasn't. I stole those cows, Hugh — and you stole them. For once, what do you say we face the truth?"

"If we hadn't picked up those Spoon critters, somebody else would have," Racklyn insisted harshly.

Overdeck shrugged. "Could very well have been. But the cold facts are — we took them. You did and I did. I'm not saying I'm sorry. I'd do the same thing over again under the circumstances. Like it or not, Racklyn, we're pretty much alike, you and me. We're two of a kind."

Racklyn dropped his hand from Overdeck's arm. What had set him off was not so much the actual content of Overdeck's words, as it was their reminding him that as of this moment, the only man of any amount on this Hatchet Rim range willing to offer him a hand was this man beside him — this man he had so long hated and still did, for that matter.

Hugh Racklyn knew he was through as far as Rufe Wilkerson was concerned. He had

236

seen that in Wilkerson's eyes, had heard it in the tone of his voice when Wilkerson had questioned him about those vented brands. He'd had no good answer to give Wilkerson then, and he had none now. For all of it he could thank Haslam, and the bile rose thick and bitter in Hugh Racklyn's throat at the mere thought of the man.

And Overdeck was right about town opinion, of course. However, Racklyn felt he'd never really had town opinion behind him, so he didn't give a damn there. It was the loss of Rufe Wilkerson's good will that hurt. Up until now, Racklyn had never realized how much it meant to him. It wasn't just that it carried with it Cora Wilkerson's friendship and regard, but there was a badge of respectability about it somehow that he needed to balance him. Now that was gone, and the loss left him queerly shaken and uncertain.

He turned back on Overdeck again, demanding, "Suppose I don't want to join up with you. What'll you do?"

"Start sitting out a few hands."

"Maybe you think I need help to take care of Haslam?"

Now it was Syl Overdeck's chance for a sarcastic moment. "How much luck have you had so far, Hugh?"

Again that wild-anger flare showed in Racklyn's eyes, but it as quickly faded. This was gall and wormwood to him, but there was an instinct stirring and lifting strongly in him, urging caution against his usual headlong, trampling way.

"You got some ideas, maybe? About Haslam, I mean?"

"Only that we do something before he gets too big," said Overdeck. "Right now there's just him and Didion and young Caddell. A week, two weeks from now, who can say? There may be half a dozen more out there riding those meadows. Like I said, time is on Haslam's side. If we intend to do anything, it better be now."

Racklyn's cigar had gone cold. He scratched a match and his cheeks caved deeply inward as he puffed the cigar to a renewed glow. He whipped the match back and forth to put it out, then as he tossed it aside, his glance boring savagely at Syl Overdeck, Hugh Racklyn made his concession.

"You could have something there. I'll warn you of one thing. You try and double-cross me and I'll hunt you down if it takes the last breath I'll ever know. Now, let's go inside and have our little talk over a drink!"

# CHAPTER X

Up on the line-backed dun horse, and leading a pair of pack animals, Riley Haslam rode from the livery corrals to Len Pechard's store. It was midmorning and the world held a fine, fresh vigor. Doc Jay, stepping from the store door, sent his big voice out in a good-natured rumble.

"Anybody would think he was set to feed an army, hauling grub by pack animals."

Haslam showed a small grin. "Grub's the least of it, Doc. Ever try moving window sashes across rough country on a pack horse? I expect this will give me gray hair."

Doc eyed Haslam keenly. "Interesting," he murmured. "I've often wondered if it could be so, and it seems to be. Maybe I'll write up my observations."

Haslam paused to spin a smoke. "I hope you know what you're talking about. I sure don't."

Doc chuckled. "Just observing the effect of circumstance on human appearance and behavior. You may not realize it, my friend, but you're a considerably different man today than you were the night you arrived here in Palisade."

"Well, I sure hope so!" exclaimed Haslam. "First time you laid eyes on me I was one sore and beat-up pilgrim. But now —" He doubled his fists, thumped himself about the ribs. "Not a squeak."

"Wasn't referring to that," Doc said. "It's what's inside the shell that interests me. You're becoming a whole man again, in a way vastly more important than just the physical. Then you were a man without purpose, without a damn thing to tie to that was worth while. Figuratively, you stood in a far corner apart from everyone else. You were suspicious, bitter and hostile; resentful of life because it was turning up increasingly empty for you. It shows in your eyes, in the cast of your head and shoulders. I'd say you'd found a new and better foundation in that pride you mentioned, the night I tied up your ribs."

Haslam, inhaling deeply, considered in quizzical silence for a moment before nodding slowly, a musing smile pulling at his lips.

"Just like you'd been studying a bug under a glass, eh, Doc? Well, I had no idea it showed up that strong, but I got to admit you've called the turn."

Doc spoke of other things. "Any sign of trouble lately from Rocking R or Two Link?" he asked.

Haslam shook his head. "All quiet out along Deer Creek. Gives Frank Didion and Bud Caddell and me a chance to fix things up around headquarters."

"Just so you don't get lulled into taking anything for granted," cautioned Doc.

"Nothing like that," Haslam told him.

Len Pechard and his wife were checking stock in the store. Cecily Pechard was a small, neat woman, and when Haslam and her storekeeper husband had gone out to the storeroom in back to look for some of the gear Haslam wanted, she fixed Doc with a bright, dark eye.

"So that's Riley Haslam, is it? He looks quite ordinary to me. Well," she amended, "maybe not quite ordinary, for there is something about him. . . . Yet, from the way that man of mine has been talking, I expected to see somebody almost half again as tall as you, Doctor, and at least twice as wide across the back."

Doc's laugh was a booming rumble. "In some ways, Cecily, maybe he is."

Outside sounded the soft mutter of hoofs,

241

coming to a stop in front of the store. Then it was the Wilkerson sisters who came in. Behind them, the compact, capable figure of Walt Heighly paused in the doorway.

Cecily Pechard exclaimed with quick pleasure. "Cora — Janet! Am I glad to see you! I'll brew a pot of coffee and we'll have a real get-together. I've been simply dying for a chance to talk to somebody besides men."

She stepped between the two girls, tucked a hand to the elbow of each, gave them an impulsive squeeze. "Oh," she said again, "it is good to see you!"

Cora Wilkerson, Doc observed, was grave and subdued-looking, a little weary about the eyes. Her voice was low as she answered Cecily Pechard.

"I'll enjoy a good visit with you, Cecily."

Janet said, "You two will have to get along without me for a little while. I'm going over to the Staghorn to say hello to Mother Orde. She'd skin me if I ever came to town and didn't drop in on her for a few minutes." She put her clear glance on Doc Jay and said, "How are you, Doctor?"

Doc, his blue eyes twinkling, bowed slightly. "Highly honored, my dear, to be virtually alone with the three prettiest ones in the whole territory. Ladies, I'm all aflutter."

"Bosh!" sniffed Cecily Pechard. Then she added, with a twinkle, "But he's a sweet old friend, just the same."

Riley Haslam came in from the storeroom, a window sash under each arm. He stopped, startled and uncertain. Doc Jay chuckled.

"They'll forgive you for not tipping your hat, my friend. They wouldn't want you to drop the sashes and spread broken glass all over the place."

Haslam, recovering, inclined his head, said, "Ladies!" and went on through. Len Pechard followed him, also lugging a pair of window sashes.

At the door, Walt Heighly, swinging aside to let Haslam pass, said, "Looks like you might be intending to build something?"

Haslam stacked the sashes carefully against a porch post before answering. Then, as he straightened up, he said, "These are to replace the windows in Scuffy Elrod's old Spoon headquarters. You ever over that way, drop in. Always glad to see friends."

Walt Heighly met Haslam's direct glance, then nodded. "That," he said, "could be so."

With Len Pechard helping, Haslam loaded the two pack horses with the window sashes and several armfuls of other supplies and gear. By the time this was done, Walt Heighly had drifted off up the street to the Staghorn bar, while Cora Wilkerson and Cecily Pechard had gone over to the Pechard home, a modest little dwelling set back from the street at the edge of the green, cool timber, and fenced about with split pickets. Janet Wilkerson, however, still lingered in the store, seemingly interested in the contents of a small showcase. But now, as Riley Haslam made a final check of his pack hitches, she came out and stood at the edge of the porch.

"I suppose," she said, "I could be called shameless or forward, or something of the sort. Yet I don't mind if you don't, for there are a couple of things I want to say to you."

Haslam smiled gravely into her clear, steady glance. "Why should I mind? If there's anything on earth I can do for you, just name it. For I owe you that and so much more."

For a moment she watched him, color stealing softly through her cheeks. This girl, he thought, this slim, straightforward girl, was the most honest thing he'd ever known or could hope to know in this world. . . .

"First," said Janet Wilkerson, "I hope you're not taking lightly that threat Hugh

Racklyn made to you. Dad told me about that, and I — well, you will be very careful, won't you?"

Haslam, still smiling, nodded. "I'm being — very careful. What else?"

"Why," she said, "I want to thank you for opening my father's eyes to the real Hugh Racklyn. You've no idea the worry that has taken off my mind."

"I wouldn't try and claim any credit there," Haslam said. "I've the feeling some pretty straight questions were demanding answers in Rufe Wilkerson's mind. Racklyn couldn't have fooled him much longer."

Janet nodded. "That may be so. But it was what you said and did that hastened the decision. Dad admits as much. So, for Dad, and for Cora, too — I thank you."

"Your sister Cora," said Haslam, "she was, well, fond of Racklyn?"

"And still is, I'm afraid," was the reluctant admission. "Dad's pretty harsh about that. I suppose you might say that I am, too, but at least I can understand how it could be. For when you care for a man, you care for him, and there isn't always a full measure of logic and balance considered."

Haslam's smile widened. "Wise," he murmured, "as a tree full of owls." Then, sobering, he added, "I can hardly claim acquaintance with your sister, but I imagine she's pretty long-headed. So I wouldn't worry too much, there."

"You don't know Wilkerson women," Janet declared. "They can be pretty skittish."

Haslam shook his head. "Not you. Not ever you."

"Maybe you're forgetting," she said. "It was night, black night. Men were fighting brutally, savagely. On some crazy impulse I go to help a man I'd never seen before, might never have seen again. If that isn't being skittish, what is?"

"It could," said Haslam, "have been an unguessed destiny moving you. There are some who scoff at the idea that destiny has anything to do with the lives of men and women. I used to scoff myself. Now, I'm not so sure."

She looked at him in a soft, still, slightly breathless manner. "How strange," she said, "that you should speak that way. For you see, the same thought came to me. About destiny, I mean. Why should you count with me, Riley Haslam — or I with you? For it is that way, isn't it?"

"Yes, it is that way." The sudden intensity in his words made them almost harsh. "I think we both understood that the other morning out at Running W headquarters."

"And you are sorry, or angry? You sound so."

He shook a decisive head. "Never sorry. But angry, yes. At myself. For wasting so many good years amounting to nothing. For allowing myself to become the kind of man I am. Girl, I've no right to even think of such as you!"

The softness in her eyes had become a glow and a dawning smile cast her lips in utter sweetness. There was a little lilt in her voice.

"Just so you care, you have every right."

She was gone then, dropping from the porch to the street and hurrying off along it in her erect, light, quick-striding way. Haslam watched her, gravely thoughtful, stirred and warmed by emotions he thought he'd long since squeezed out of his life.

Behind him, from the doorway of the store, Doc Jay said, "The bug under the glass grows more interesting all the time."

Without looking that way Haslam said, a slight edge to his voice, "You wouldn't be playing a prying old woman, would you, Doc?"

Doc gave out his rumbling chuckle. "A man has few secrets from his doctor."

Haslam shook his head, mollified. "Am I that easy to read?"

"The harder the crust on a man, the more revealing it is when broken," said Doc. "And there are some things, when they come to a man, that awaken a shine in him. My friend, I'd have to be stony blind not to see this in you. Now, for the Lord's sake, don't start building up a lot of stupid obstacles that actually exist only in your mind. Remember, life was made to be grabbed with both hands, not picked at cautiously from a distance. Bless your good fortune that a girl like Janet Wilkerson sees fit to look on you kindly. Few men are that lucky."

Haslam smiled faintly, jeering. "The old philosopher himself."

Doc shrugged. "In this world, my friend, you must be somewhat of a philosopher to keep your sanity and sense of proportion. Else the accumulation of human stupidity will convince you that man is creation's biggest mistake."

Haslam's smile widened to a grin as he turned his near stirrup, toed it and went into the saddle. "How the man does run on! He's beginning to get almost weighty. Which makes it time for me to get out of here."

He stirred the dun to movement and with the two pack horses at lead, rode south out of town.

Cory Biggs, an arm in a sling, stepped out of Doc Jay's quarters into the sunlight's warmth and shine. Both were vital and good, and he paused there under their benevolence. He was thin, and a pallor lay under the weathering of his skin. He spoke with some awkwardness and hesitation.

"You've been awful damn good to me, Doc. Next payday I'll be around to see you."

Doc, leaning in the doorway, said, "No rush. I'll split the bill with you if you show some sense."

Biggs turned and blinked at Doc, bewildered. "Split the bill? I don't know what you mean, Doc."

"Just what I said. You show some sense, I'll cut the bill in half."

Cory Biggs blinked again. "What would you call showing some sense?"

"Cutting loose from Rocking R," Doc said bluntly.

"But that's my hire, that's my job," Biggs protested.

"I'm all for a man being faithful to his hire," said Doc dryly, "so long as the hire is faithful to him. Ask yourself if that's been true in your case, Biggs. Hugh Racklyn knows what happened to you, where you've been. Has he been in to see you or show you the slightest concern? No! Wake up, man! Hugh Racklyn doesn't give one thin damn about you, once you're no longer any use to him. I even doubt there's a job waiting for you out at Rocking R any more, what with you laid up with an arm that's not going to be of much use to you for another month or six weeks."

Cory Biggs shook his head. "You're wrong there, Doc. Hugh wouldn't do that to me. I got hurt fightin' for him. No, he wouldn't saw me off that way."

Doc shrugged. "Good luck!"

Cory Biggs made the ride out to Rocking R headquarters a slow one, both to keep from jolting his arm and because it took less effort to stay up on a slow-moving mount, and right now Biggs had no strength to waste.

At Rocking R, when he came up past the corrals, Hugh Racklyn stepped from the ranch house, stood for a moment staring, then came across the interval. There was a beading of the sweat of weakness across Biggs's upper lip, and his smile was a little wan.

"Hello, Hugh," he said. "A bad penny turned up again. Wonder would you have one of the other boys unsaddle this bronc for me. I'm not quite up to the chore just yet."

"How long," demanded Racklyn, "do you figure to be laid up with that arm?"

"Doc Jay said a month or six weeks."

"Then," said Racklyn, brutally blunt, "there's no need to unsaddle the horse. Because you're riding out again. If you got any personal gear in the bunkhouse, go collect it while I make out your time."

Cory Biggs sagged in his saddle. "You — you mean you're lettin' me go, Hugh?"

"What else?"

"But I got this — this arm, fighting for Rocking R. And —"

"You could have got it by getting drunk and falling off a horse, too," cut in Racklyn ruthlessly. "You think I can afford to have saddle hands laying around for six weeks doing nothing but drawing wages and eating their heads off? Like hell! I'm not made of money. Go get your gear!"

Racklyn went back to the ranch house. Cory Biggs slid from his saddle, stood for an unsteady moment or two, using the support of his horse's shoulder while getting the feel of the earth under his feet again. Then he crossed slowly over and into the bunkhouse.

The bunk he'd once slept in was stripped of blankets. His few personal effects were pushed under it. The bunkhouse held a single occupant besides himself, a grizzled, time-warped rider named Albie Tharp, who was repairing a bridle. As Cory Biggs dragged his war bag from under the bunk and began stuffing odds and ends of gear into it, Tharp spoke up, his voice low and dry.

"Getting smart, eh Biggs? Quitting this damned layout?"

"Not quitting. Fired. Hugh's making out my time now."

"Just couldn't stand the thought of paying you wages and feeding you while you were getting back on your feet, is that it?"

Biggs nodded. "That's what he said. I — I didn't figger Hugh Racklyn that way."

Albie Tharp laughed thinly and without mirth. "Live and learn, Biggs. At that, you're lucky. You're getting away from this outfit while you're still alive. Which is more than some of the rest of us will do."

Cory Biggs's head came up. "Don't get you, Tharp. What do you mean?"

The seamed and grizzled oldster brought out tobacco and papers and built a cigarette before answering. Then, as he lipped and lighted this, he looked through the smoke at Biggs.

"How did you get that arm, Biggs? By fighting Two Link. Now, so help me, Syl Overdeck and Hugh Racklyn have turned thick as thieves. That's right. I saw it with my own eyes. Syl Overdeck rode in here and Racklyn invited him into the ranch house. One of the boys who happened to get a good look through a window said they were having a drink together."

"That is hard to believe," said Biggs.

Albie Tharp shrugged. "Ain't it, though! If I hadn't seen it, I'd be hard to convince, too. Now, there had to be a reason, and there is. This feller Haslam. He's dug in along Deer Creek. Rocking R and Two Link are combining to root him out. Both outfits are riding to hit him tonight, no holds barred."

He inhaled deeply, then went on. "So, this outfit's had men killed, fighting against Two Link. Hodgy got killed doing that, while you picked up that arm in the same ruckus. Now there's liable to be Rocking R men killed, fighting for Two Link. For with Racklyn and Overdeck throwing in together on this soiree, you can't fight for Rocking R without fighting for Two Link. It don't make sense." Albie Tharp took another drag at his cigarette before adding, "The older you get, the less sense it makes, just riding wild and putting your life on the line because a feller like Hugh Racklyn orders it that way. You should be glad you're cutting loose from it, Biggs."

Cory Biggs looked at the old fellow wonderingly. There had been a vast and caustic bitterness in Albie Tharp's final words, reflecting the weary disillusionment of too many empty years, and the bleakness of a corroding wisdom.

"Feeling that way, Albie, you ought to quit," said Biggs. "Why don't you?"

Again Albie Tharp showed that thin and mirthless laugh and he lifted a hand to touch his grizzled hair. "At my age, for the privilege of eating regular, and sleeping under a roof, you're willing to gamble against the chance of stopping a slug. Besides, there's not too much time left, anyhow, so it don't really matter. No, quitting a job is a luxury to be enjoyed while you're young."

Biggs went on packing his war bag. But there was something missing. He looked at Albie Tharp again. "I had a spare six-shooter once. Ain't here now."

Albie Tharp threw back a corner of the blankets of his bunk, produced the weapon and handed it over. "Glad you remembered. I'd about forgot. First word we got after that ruckus with Two Link in the Deer Creek Meadows was that you were dead. The boys were set to divide up your stuff. I hid that gun out on them."

There were some loose cartridges in his gear, so holding the gun between his knees, Biggs one-handedly opened the loading gate, slipped a load into five of the chambers, set the hammer on the empty sixth one and tucked the gun down inside the waistband of his jeans, under the flap of his jumper.

Albie Tharp, watching this, said, "Ain't aiming to go hostile on anybody, are you?"

Cory Biggs shrugged. "No use owning an empty gun. Obliged, Albie, for keeping the gun for me."

Now it was Tharp who shrugged. "Alive, it's still yours. If you'd been dead, well, I could have sold it somewhere for the price of a good drunk. Luck!"

Carrying his war bag, Cory Biggs went out. It was a little rough, working with one hand, to get the gear slung to his saddle, but he managed it finally, and then crawled astride. When he reined over to the ranch house, Hugh Racklyn came across the porch and handed up a few coins. Biggs spread the coins on his palm, stared at them. They represented about half of what he felt he had coming. Quick anger stirred in him and his head came up. He found Racklyn watching him narrowly.

"That squares us, doesn't it, Biggs?" Racklyn demanded. "I figure it does."

Heated retort hung on Cory Biggs's lips, but he held it back. He'd like to have told Hugh Racklyn many things, but he didn't. For now, as he had this good, measuring look at the man, he recognized the deep change that had taken place. The cast of Racklyn's face had sagged, somehow, and his features coarsened to a brutal heaviness. The wildness always promised by the lines about his mouth was loose and flickering in his eyes. The man was openly dangerous. Here was a time for caution, and Cory Biggs observed it. He pocketed the coins, shrugged and reined away. He moved into the timber and on to the town trail, which wound its way along the narrow river flats.

By the time Cory Biggs got back to Palisade, he knew what he was going to do. He skirted town, hit the eastbound trail just south of town and turned into it. He was surprised at how much better he felt than when he'd first got into the saddle this day. Stirring around helped, he guessed, and no doubt the queer uplift he knew over his now-determined moves had something to do with it. In any event, he was a better and more capable man than he'd been a few hours ago.

There was nothing outstanding about Cory Biggs, either in looks or make-up. His present determination was actuated fully as much by his feeling of vindictiveness toward Hugh Racklyn as it was by gratitude toward Riley Haslam. Yet this last did count.

For Biggs was remembering that day in the Deer Creek Meadows. Sure, it had been Haslam who had sent a rifle bullet crashing into his arm, a bullet that Haslam openly admitted he'd intended for a more fatal purpose. Yet, when the fight was over and done with, Haslam had shown him gruff consideration, had been ready to make a lone-handed shootout of it with Syl Overdeck and Ben Spawn, rather than let these two have their way with him. And after that, Haslam had seen to it that he reached Palisade and professional care by Doc Jay.

You couldn't, Biggs told himself, plumb overlook a break like that. For, while he owed this crippled arm to Haslam, he also owed the fact that he was alive this minute. On the other hand, what had Racklyn done for him? Short-changed him on wages due, given him a raw deal all around. Treated him like he was of no more concern than nothing. Which he was, in Racklyn's eyes. Nobody was, except Racklyn himself.

The Rocking R hands, how about them?

Did he owe them anything? Not a damn thing that he knew of, decided Biggs. The outfit had always been that way. It was rough and tough and you held up your end by yourself, for you could bet nobody would be there to help. How much had any of them given a damn while he was laid up? They'd found out that he wasn't dead, that he was laid up with a bad arm at Doc Jay's quarters. But had any called around to see him? None. But when they first thought him dead, they were ready to paw his gear over and divide it up, like, thought Biggs bitterly, a flock of buzzards working over a dead carcass.

No, he owed nothing to anyone out at Rocking R, nothing except this chance to get even with Hugh Racklyn, and that he was going to do, so far as he was able. Now he recognized what a break of fortune it had been that Albie Tharp had been in the Rocking R bunkhouse, and that the old-timer had been bitter and in the mood to unburden himself. But for that, there'd have been no word to carry to Riley Haslam. Well, thought Biggs, all of a man's luck couldn't be bad.

The trail broke from the thicker timber, ran through the thinning fringe, where the lava began thrusting up in black and tumbled piles. And then there showed the new green of the aspens and the willows, and the trail dipped across the low slope to the river ford, and the voice of the water was a steady, tumultuous rushing.

Breaking through the willows, Cory Biggs pulled up at the river's edge for his look at the crossing and then, as his horse showed its desire with a thrusting head, he let the reins fall slack so that the animal might move a stride or two into the water and then drop its head to drink. And it was at this moment that Ben Spawn rode into view on the far bank.

With only a split second of pause, the Two Link foreman set his mount to the crossing and came surging straight for Cory Biggs, the water rolling away before the thrust of his horse's chest. Ben Spawn rode high and alert in his saddle, and his glance, fixed on Cory Biggs, was hard with suspicion. Spawn drove past the main core of the current and then, where it was quieter near the western bank, he pulled up but a few yards distant from Biggs. His rasping, gravelly voice hit out above the sound of the river.

"Just where the hell do you think you're going?"

Cory Biggs had no good or immediate

answer to this. He might have had, but for one thing. The war bag lashed to his saddle. That was open advertisement that he was done up at Rocking R, that he was on his own, on the move. Only two places he'd be heading for along this trail. Either Two Link — or Spoon headquarters on Deer Creek. What possible reason for him heading for Two Links? There was none. But at Spoon . . .

Biggs had the feeling that Ben Spawn's hard stare was cutting right through all barriers and reading his thoughts. A small and desperate panic settled and grew in him. It took all the will power he possessed to lift his head and hold Spawn's glance. But he still could find no sound answer to give, so he remained silent. Spawn moved his horse a stride closer, stabbed a pointing finger at Biggs's war bag.

"You must be through at Rocking R, else you wouldn't be lugging that. When did you pull out from there?"

Cory Biggs thought Ben Spawn's voice the roughest he had ever heard. It had an overpowering insistence that dragged a blurted answer from him.

"Today. Couple hours ago. Racklyn let me go because of this arm. Said he didn't want me laying around eating my head off and doing nothing."

Biggs cupped his right hand under the sling-supported left arm, lifting it a trifle to ease it. And with the move he felt the hard butt of the gun tucked in the waistband of his jeans and hidden from sight by the flap of his jumper. Damned if he hadn't half forgotten about that gun! He sat a little straighter in his saddle, and kept his right hand where it was.

Ben Spawn threw another question at him. "You hear any talk out at Rocking R?"

Cory Biggs, a new, small gleam of courage stirring in him because of that gun, answered with a question of his own.

"What kind of talk you mean, Spawn? What kind of talk would there have been besides what Racklyn made when he give me my time?"

It was a fairly good try at evasion, and it might have worked on someone less suspicious than Spawn. But Spawn had been asking several silent questions, as well as his spoken ones. This fellow Biggs was through at Rocking R. And only two possible destinations lay ahead of him out this trail. Two Link certainly wouldn't be the one. It had to be Spoon. And why Spoon?

The suspicion in Ben Spawn's eyes deepened and the unraveling of his line of probing thought quickened. Spoon had to be where Biggs was heading. And in his present shape, Biggs was of no use as a rider or for any other kind of chore around a ranch. Biggs admitted he'd just been given his time at Rocking R a couple of hours ago, which meant he hadn't expected to leave there. And now, right away, he was heading for Spoon!

Suspicion became conviction in Ben Spawn's mind and he made a small, unconscious shift in his saddle which told its own story to Cory Biggs, and Biggs knew he had only one possible answer to the final question Spawn threw at him.

"You damn sure you didn't talk to anybody but Racklyn, out at Rocking R?"

Cory Biggs, in trapped desperation, gave his answer. His right hand slid under the flap of his jumper, came away weighted with blue-black gun metal. And Ben Spawn, his right shoulder dipping a trifle to the move, was drawing at the same time.

The hard cough of gun report spread to a spattering echo across the river ford. A massive blow hit Cory Biggs in the chest, carrying with it a deep and savage agony, driving him reeling far back in his saddle, his face tipped to the sky. His own weapon, lifting with the move, blasted its report in blind reaction, and again the shuddering echoes rocketed above the ford.

In Ben Spawn's forehead, just under the down-pulled brim of his hat, a round blue hole appeared, and his hat, lifting in the back, shifted slightly on his head. Then Spawn was falling, toppling stiffly like a felled tree might. Head and shoulders struck the river waters first, for his foot hung up in the near stirrup for a moment. But the startled whirl of his horse jerked this loose and then the current had free use of Spawn, and it rolled him over and over and then drew him from sight into a chute of deeper water, swirling and plunging under the overhanging mass of willows. Only his hat remained in sight, caught on a snag at the willows' edge.

Like Spawn's horse, Cory Biggs's mount swung away from the blasting of gunfire virtually in its face. It splashed from the shallows back up the west bank, and it was here that Cory Biggs, rolling and wobbling loosely in his saddle, finally slid free of it, to lie crumpled and still in the trail. And that was the way Walt Heighly, jogging along this trail five minutes later, found him.

# CHAPTER XI

At Spoon Headquarters, all was work and sweat. The window sashes that Riley Haslam had brought out from town the day before had been fitted in place, and the new lumber looked almost white against the weathered material surrounding it. Now, along with Frank Didion and Bud Caddell, Haslam was digging holes and setting posts for a new corral. It was Frank Didion, pausing to scrub the sweat from his face, who glanced down the meadow, then gave low-voiced but crisp warning.

"Heads up!"

Riley Haslam straightened, had his look and said, "It's all right. That's Walt Heighly of Running W."

Haslam moved out a little way to meet the oncoming rider, who was approaching at a fast jog. Haslam knew a swift touch of pleasure, for he liked this quiet, steady fellow who was the ramrod of Running W; liked the way he looked you in the eye, the way he stood by his convictions, and how his judgment of men worked out sound and correct.

As Heighly reined to a stop, Haslam lifted a hand in greeting. "Light down, friend," he invited. "Glad you dropped by. We'll be setting out some grub, shortly."

Heighly stepped from his saddle and then, as he stood fully facing him, Haslam recognized a sober gravity in this man. His query was swift.

"Something wrong, Heighly? Out at Running W, maybe?"

Heighly nodded. "Wrong — but not at Running W. This could be a great break of luck for you, Haslam, my getting the idea to ride out here today."

Haslam stared at him. "I don't know what you mean, but you evidently do. Let's hear it."

Walt Heighly told his story with curt bluntness. In town on some business for Rufe Wilkerson, he'd decided to go home the roundabout way, circling out through the lavas to Spoon headquarters, then cutting back to cross the river again below Rocking R and hit the home trail from there. And just a little bit ago, on his way out to this spot, back by the river ford, he'd come across Cory Biggs laying in the trail, shot through and through, and dying.

"Cory Biggs!" exclaimed the startled

Haslam. "What would he have been doing there, and who —"

"Get to that in a minute," cut in Heighly. "Now I just happened to have a pint of liquor in my saddle bags that I'd picked up in town for old Judey Mills, our ranch cook, who don't get to town very often and who likes a little nip of mornings. So, when I saw Biggs was still alive, I poured a good jolt of that liquor into him, and it brought him back far enough so that he recognized me and could talk some."

Heighly reached over, lifted Haslam's sack of tobacco from his shirt pocket, built and lit a cigarette. After his first big inhalation, he went on.

"Make what you want of this, Haslam, but this is what Biggs told me. Doc Jay turned him loose this morning and he rode out to Rocking R, figuring he still belonged to Racklyn's outfit. He was wrong. Racklyn not only gave him his time, but shorted him on wages. While Biggs was getting his gear together, one of the Rocking R hands let it slip that Racklyn and Syl Overdeck have smoked the peace pipe and joined forces to run you out of the picture. They're going to hit you tonight, no holds barred. Biggs, figuring he owed you something because you treated him decent, while Racklyn hadn't,

266

was on his way out there to tip you off. But he bumped into Ben Spawn at the river ford, and Spawn shot him."

"Ben Spawn did? The devil!"

"Yeah," affirmed the Running W foreman. "Ben Spawn did. But Biggs got off a shot himself, and did a better job of it than he knew. For another horse with an empty saddle was there besides the one Biggs had ridden. It carried the Two Link brand. I started looking around and saw a hat caught on a willow snag a little down stream from the ford. I went around below there where a fast-running pool tapers up to a shallows. A man was jammed up in the shallows. It was Ben Spawn and he had a bullet hole almost square between the eyes."

"I will be damned!" exclaimed Haslam. "What else, Walt?"

Heighly shrugged. "You've had it, all of it. I dragged Spawn out on the bank and went back to Biggs. He was dead. So I moved both him and Spawn back into the willows out of sight of the trail. I tied the two horses out of sight, too, then came on out here. There it is. You take it from here."

Riley Haslam stared off across the meadow to where the far edge lifted to meet the lava badlands. His face was hard-pulled, and little knots of muscle crawled and bunched at the corners of his jaw.

"I wouldn't try and deny the word of a dead man," he said presently. "Especially when he'd died trying to get that word to me. But it's hard to believe that Racklyn and Overdeck would ever join forces for any reasons. Hell! Anybody would think Riley Haslam was an army, instead of just one lone, damned ordinary man."

"May appear that way," Heighly said, "but there's another way to look at it. Like this. Maybe it's not so much what you actually are, as what you represent. Which is the first really active opposition Hugh Racklyn and Syl Overdeck, aside from their own private squabble, have run up against. You make even a halfway showing in that opposition, you'll encourage others to try the same. And Racklyn and Overdeck can afford that even less than fighting each other. Yeah, to Racklyn and Overdeck, you and what you represent are a dangerous idea."

Haslam shook his head ruefully. "I sure didn't set out to cut that wide a trail." Then he added, softly, "That Cory Biggs! Just because I treated him like a human being, after wrecking an arm for him, he goes all out to bring me a warning. You just never know about a man."

"I remember a grandmother of mine," said Heighly. "She doted on her Bible and was always quoting it. She had a favorite that was about 'bread cast upon waters.' I reckon that comes up true, every now and then."

Haslam made a slow, complete turn, his glance running far and speculative. "So it's to be tonight, eh? And we're to get everything, no holds barred. Well, it could turn out interesting."

"You're not figuring to make a stand of it here, are you?" Heighly demanded quickly.

"Why not?" shrugged Haslam. "It all boils down to one of two choices. Either I stand, or run. I'm not going to run. And for a stand, this is as good a place as any. Oh, I'll make the kid, Bud Caddell, clear out. He's a good lad and I don't want him mixed in with what could be a mean mess. With Didion and me, it's different. We've been over the jumps before. So knowing what to expect, it will be a damned strange thing if Frank and I can't cook up a pretty fair chunk of trouble."

"But you said it just now," protested Heighly. "That you're no army. It still stands, even with a fellow like Didion to side you. You'll be outnumbered, five or six to one."

"Probably," agreed Haslam. "But the advantage of surprise and position will be with Frank and me. That counts, too."

Walt Heighly turned back to his horse. "I admire your guts, but not your judgment, Haslam. Thanks for the invite to grub, but I'd better get along. For I've got to go back to town now and tell Doc Jay about those two out at the river ford. He generally looks after such things. Better think it over, friend. I still say you'd be smart to play the shifty fox instead of the stubborn bear. Good luck!"

Haslam watched the Running W foreman ride away, then turned and went back to where Frank Didion and Bud Caddell waited curiously. "This," he said, bluntly slow, "will jolt you." He went on to tell of the word Walt Heighly had brought. Bud Caddell caught his breath.

"Yeah, kid," said Haslam, looking at him. "That's how rough this kind of game can get. And it's no place for you. So you saddle up and git! As of this minute, you're fired. In town, you drop in and tell Cash Fletcher I said to pay you ten days' wages."

The wave of color that swept across Bud's face was a mixture of hurt surprise and a slow realizing anger.

"That I'm good enough to work for

Spoon but not good enough to fight for it, is what you're telling me?" he demanded.

Haslam shrugged. "If it sounds that way, then I guess that's it."

Bud's voice thickened with emotion. "I can put up a fight. I'm not afraid. There's no streak in me. Be damned if I'll leave!"

Haslam kept his expression unreadable, and his tone and words ran harshly blunt. "You heard what I said. Climb your saddle and get out of here!"

Bud's face began to work a little. "Hell with you!" he cried. He had a shovel in his hands. He threw this aside and turned away. "Yeah — hell with you!"

He caught and saddled and headed out without another word or backward look. Frank Didion spoke softly.

"I know exactly why you did that, Riley. But couldn't you have softened it a little? He's a good lad."

Haslam, looking after Bud Caddell, a gray regret in his eyes, nodded. "Sure he's a good lad. None better. Too good and too young for me to let him chance stopping a slug. Don't think I enjoyed playing rough with him, because I didn't. Yet I had to make it that way or he'd never have gone. There'll come a time when he'll thank me. Now, how about you, Frank? This thing could

271

shape up meaner than anything we ever went through together before. And I'm not holding you to a thing."

"Didn't I tell you once that I'd given up any idea of riding across the mountains alone?" said Didion steadily. "Well, that's it! So suppose we get down to figuring just how we're going to play this little game tonight."

Cora Wilkerson had dressed herself for riding and had Mitch Connerly catch and saddle for her. And when Janet caught up with her on the ranch house porch, an anxious question in her eyes, Cora shook her head.

"I'm not going against Dad's orders, Baby. If I intended to, I'd tell him beforehand. And I don't want you with me, either. I don't want anybody with me. I've some things to straighten out in my mind, once and for all, and I've got to be alone to do it. Now don't worry about me."

An hour later, Cora rode into Palisade. She had not had this destination consciously in mind, for she had told Janet the truth when she voiced her need to be alone while threshing out some sort of sound answer to the problems vexing her. Of these, the central one was Hugh Racklyn.

There was no use denying she'd been fond of him, and still was. Just how truly deep the feeling went was what she wasn't sure of and, more than any other thing, this was the answer she had to have. She had taken her father's admonition about ever seeing Racklyn again, silently, but with reservations. She was no child. She was a young woman grown, with the right to judge her own life and future.

Her father's flat statement that Hugh Racklyn was a cattle thief had shaken her badly. To see her father swing abruptly from friendship with Racklyn to a position of open hostility was even a greater shock. For she knew her father, knew the streak of uncompromising honesty in him, when once aroused. He was not the sort to judge any man so harshly unless convinced beyond all doubt that he was right.

Yet, because she wished it might be so, she clung to a small remnant of hope that her father might be mistaken. Or that at least there existed some mitigating circumstances for what Racklyn had done.

All the way to town, Cora wrestled with these hopes and doubts, yet, when she rode into town she was no closer to a satisfactory answer to any of them than when she'd left home. Habit, more than anything else, made her pull up and dismount at the rail of Len Pechard's general store. As long as she was here, she might as well see if there was any mail. And maybe Cecily Pechard might be on hand, to visit with a little.

There was another horse tied at the hitch rail, but Cora paid it no attention. And then, as she crossed the store porch, it was Hugh Racklyn who stepped from the open door. He was startled as she, and for a moment he seemed at a loss of what to do or say. Then he touched his hat brim and blurted, "Hello, Cora."

For a little time she did not answer, just standing there, looking at him, seeing things which startled and shocked her. This man was changed. Once she had thought him handsome in a strong, virile sort of way. But now there was a coarseness in his face, and that wild flaring in his eyes. Some inner ferment was burning this man up.

Marking her hesitation, her startled scrutiny, Racklyn's lips showed a heavy, sardonic curl. "What have they been telling you about me, Cora? Remember, we were pretty good friends, once. I'm still the same man. Are you still the same girl?"

Cora said nothing aloud. But inwardly she was crying, "You're not the same man. Something rather dreadful has happened to you. You've let go of all pretense of respectability. You're a stranger, and I don't know you — nor want to —"

She pulled her eyes away from him, looked along the street. Angling down from the Staghorn came a shuffling, twisted figure. It was Scuffy Elrod, carrying a market basket on his arm. Cora had heard the story about Scuffy Elrod, of the accident that had made him what he was. And once she had heard a whisper that she had heatedly and vehemently denied at the time; a whisper that it had not been an accident with Scuffy Elrod, that it had been a deliberate effort at Elrod's life, while made to look accidental. And Cora had denied this the way she had, because that whisper also contained the name of Hugh Racklyn. The whisper also said that whenever Scuffy Elrod happened to be anywhere near Hugh Racklyn, he cowered like a dog that had been whipped past all endurance.

Cora had flatly refused to believe the whisper and for that reason, until now, she had almost forgotten it. But here, watching Scuffy Elrod approach, she wondered, a coldness beginning to settle in the pit of her stomach. She had to fight a little to hold her voice steady.

"Why, yes — I have been hearing things,

Hugh. I'd like to believe they weren't true. Are they?"

He laughed, a little roughly. "Not knowing what the things are, how can I say? Yet if you weren't already pretty well convinced, you wouldn't ask me. Would it do me any good to deny them?"

Scuffy Elrod had reached the edge of the store porch. Now he came along it, a gray, weathered, cruelly twisted little man, apparently completely locked away from the world in some mental sphere all his own. As he drew closer, his faded glance touched Cora, held steady and unchanged until it went past her to Hugh Racklyn. Then, instantly, it was different.

Cora, watching, saw the raw and naked fear which leaped into Scuffy Elrod's eyes. She thought she had never seen fear like that before. Only one thing could have produced it — some past terror and cruelty almost beyond measure. Cowering, Scuffy Elrod dodged into the store.

Standing very straight, her arms stiffly at her sides, Cora Wilkerson found final answer to her problem. She spoke quite steadily, but as though from a great distance.

"No, Hugh. It wouldn't do you any good to deny them. No good at all. Because they're true — all of them. I can see that, now."

Down the street, it was Walt Heighly who stepped from Doc Jay's office, swung astride his waiting horse and came along at a fast jog. When even with the store, the Running W foreman slowed his pace, startled at what he saw and heard. For one thing, he saw Hugh Racklyn staring at him with an ugly but guardedly controlled malevolence. He also saw Cora Wilkerson hurriedly freeing her tethered horse, and heard her clear, glad call to him.

"Wait for me, Walt! I want to ride with you."

Walt Heighly said no word until they were clear of town. Then he asked, "Is any of it my business, Cora? You weren't supposed to see that fellow again, you know. Your father won't be happy about it."

"Oh, but he will!"' declared Cora. Her cheeks were flushed and a new vitality seemed to be coursing through her. "Yes," she said again. "Dad will be happy about it. Because it answers a question I simply had to know about. Now, I will never see Hugh Racklyn again — not in the way I used to. Does that make sense, Walt?"

He looked over at her. "It makes mighty welcome sense to me."

Her smile was warm. "I want it to, especially for you, Walt."

Back at the store, Hugh Racklyn stayed there on the porch, his thoughts lost in dark absorption while he built and smoked a cigarette. The heaviness of his features seemed to increase. Little fires were burning far back in his eyes when he finally sought his horse and rode out of town.

Barely had he left than Bud Caddell came into the southern end of the street and rode up as far as the Staghorn. As Bud dismounted and tied, Doc Jay came from his office and went into the Staghorn just a stride ahead of Bud. Inside the place, Doc stopped, for Bud had called to him.

"I want to see you, Doc. And I want to see Fletcher and everybody else in this damn town who are sittin' back letting a good man take the rough edge for them."

Doc looked at Bud gravely. "Think I know what you're driving at, son. If I'm right, you're jumping at conclusions. Give us time, boy — give us time." He turned to the bartender. "Where's Cash, Pete?"

Pete jerked an indicating head toward the stairs leading up to the balcony. "Catching a few winks against another night of late play, I think."

Doc took Bud Caddell by the arm.

"Come along and get it off your chest."

Cash Fletcher answered Doc's knock with an invitation to enter. Fletcher was seated on the edge of his bunk, just awakened and yawning. He straightened and grew more alert at the expression on Doc's face. "What's up?" he asked.

Doc tipped his head toward Bud Caddell. "First, let's listen to what the kid here has to say. He's bustin' to get rid of it."

"Tonight," blurted Bud. "They're going to hit tonight! Racklyn and Overdeck. They're joining forces to push Riley Haslam out of Deer Creek Meadows. And there's just him and Frank Didion out there to try and stand those two outfits off. It was you fellers who got Haslam to go out there in the first place. You going to sit back and let him take all the weight?"

As the import of Bud's words sunk home, Cash Fletcher hit his feet. "Making no flat statements, understand," he said curtly. "But that's pretty hard to believe. That Hugh Racklyn and Syl Overdeck would ever join up for anything."

"Maybe hard to believe, Cash — but evidently true," said Doc Jay. "Listen to the word Walt Heighly brought me." Doc went on to tell of two dead men lying out by the Cold River ford, and of the word one of them had given Walt Heighly before dying. Doc turned to Bud Caddell and added, "Heighly took the same word out to Spoon headquarters, didn't he, kid?"

"That's right, he did," said Bud. "Now what you fellers going to do about it?"

Cash Fletcher's tone went a trifle harsh. "Haslam send you in here to ask us that?"

"Not him! I came on my own. You know what Haslam did? He fired me! Told me to saddle up and get out. Acted real tough about it. At first I didn't think straight and was burned, plenty! But pretty soon I got my thinking sorted out. Reason he acted that way was to make sure I didn't get hurt; he didn't want me in the ruckus at all. Well, it ain't going to do him any good. If I can work for Spoon, I can fight for it. I'm going to be out there along Deer Creek tonight, taking my cut at any Rockin' R or Two Link jingos who show. Riley Haslam won't know about it, but I'm going to be there!"

"And not alone, kid," rumbled Doc quietly. "In my time I've dug lead out of quite a number, and sewed up and bandaged together a lot more. Tonight I'm going to do my damnedest to reverse the process. Cash, how many can we get together?"

Fletcher calculated quickly. "You and me to begin with. Len Pechard would gladly go, but Len is just simply no hand at all at that sort of thing, so we'll leave him out. I'm pretty sure if we lay it on the line with Sam Basile, he'll sit in. Then there's Pete Loftus, my bartender. Lot of salt in Pete, once you get him going. That makes four of us, and if Caddell rides with us, it'll be five. That should help." He looked at Bud. "What do you think?"

Bud flushed. "Guess I was yellin' before I knew what for. Sorry I showed up so wringy. Might have known you fellers wouldn't let Haslam down."

Doc dropped a hand on Bud's shoulder. "You're not being exactly small about it yourself, son. Well, now that we know what we'll be doing later tonight, I better take care of a mean chore. I got to go out to the ford after a couple of dead men. I'll need a little help. Feel up to it, Bud?"

Bud nodded. "In this world you got to grow up in spite of yourself."

Out at Running W headquarters, Rufe Wilkerson stood in the late afternoon sunlight and listened to what Walt Heighly had to say. Wilkerson's glance was fixed on the distant black rampart of Hatchet Rim and was as darkly frowning as the rim itself.

"I've always been a firm believer in minding my own affairs, Walt," he said.

"And I can't see where this is any of our business."

"Maybe not directly," admitted Heighly. "But indirectly it could be — plenty! Look at the odds against Haslam. He aims to make a fight of it, and it'll probably be a good one. Yet as things stand I can't see him winning it. So then Racklyn and Overdeck have the meadows. They're top dogs. Where's that liable to leave you? I'll tell you, Rufe. You and Overdeck have always been at outs. Not too long ago you read Racklyn off. So now, after they've taken care of Haslam, just where do you think Racklyn and Overdeck are liable to look next? It could be right at Running W!"

"You're reaching a long way and borrowing a lot of 'maybe' trouble, Walt. Those two won't be riding shoulder to shoulder very long. They'll be back at each other's throats wilder than ever.

"I'm not so sure of that," said Heighly thoughtfully. "Particularly if they make this raid tonight a good one. They'll have learned something, which is, together they can do a lot of things they couldn't do alone. Well, Rufe, I can't make up your mind for you. So I'll tell you this. I've talked things over with Mitch Connerly. Mitch thinks like I do, that Running W has a stake in this deal and should do something about it. So Mitch and I, come full dark, are going to be drifting in somewhere around Deer Creek Meadows."

A stubborn flush darkened Rufe Wilkerson's leathery face. Then a grim and grudging smile showed. "If you and Mitch are dead set on going, Walt — I can't stop you. In which case, I reckon I better ride along just to see that you don't get plumb to your necks in trouble. And you could be right. Maybe this is our fight as well as Haslam's."

# CHAPTER XII

Night's first early deep and velvet dark had begun to pale somewhat under the mounting pressure of the steadily massing stars, which laid a thin and deceptive glow across the world. And where open sunlight during daytime often seemed to deepen and intensify the somber shading of Hatchet Rim, this star glow traced softening highlights, and spread a sheen of foxfire across the rim face that seemed to weave and flow like liquid silver.

Standing in the flat interval halfway between ranch house and corrals out at the Two Link headquarters, Syl Overdeck saw all of this, yet saw none of it, for his jumpy thoughts were elsewhere, and his nerves thin and drawn. Where, he asked himself again, in hell was Ben Spawn?

It was a question he'd considered a dozen times in the past couple of hours, and was no closer to an answer now than then. Much earlier in the day, Ben Spawn had headed for town, to kill some time there while he looked and listened and observed. To see if he could run across any hint anywhere that word of the impending raid on Spoon headquarters had leaked out.

This had been Spawn's own idea, for he'd been against the deal with Hugh Racklyn from the first. He'd argued that point with Overdeck, stating heatedly and flatly that he wouldn't trust Racklyn as far as he could spit.

It would, Spawn had argued, be just like Racklyn to let loose a hint of the raid so that it would be sure to reach Riley Haslam's ears in time for Haslam to recruit help and get set for trouble. And then, instead of coming down from the north as planned and carry out his half of the agreed-upon attack, sit back and let Two Link come up from the south and ride straight into something that could wipe them out. Something like that, Ben Spawn had insisted, was what they might expect from Hugh Racklyn and his Rocking R.

In their initial argument, Overdeck had not agreed with Spawn at all. He had still felt it was a smart move on his part to bury the hatchet with Rocking R, at least for the present, while they disposed of Riley Haslam. But Ben Spawn's argument had placed an unsettling kernel of doubt in Overdeck's sly and conniving mind, and this had taken on swift root and growth. Now, with every passing moment, that doubt was growing bigger and bigger.

Syl Overdeck slammed a clenched fist into the open palm of his other hand. Where was Ben Spawn? What was keeping him? The thought struck that maybe Spawn, because he didn't agree with the idea of the raid under planned conditions, was going to sit it out in town. But immediately Overdeck discarded this surmise. Ben Spawn was dedicated to the welfare of Two Link; he'd proven this in a hundred different ways over the past years. No, Spawn would ride wherever Two Link rode, regardless.

But he wasn't here, and if Two Link was going to saddle and move out to do their part at Deer Creek Meadows, it was time they got started. Syl Overdeck knew he wouldn't start without Ben Spawn. It was at a time like this when he realized how much Spawn's presence meant to him, for Ben Spawn was the one man and the only man whose full fidelity to Two Link interests he could depend on utterly. And that sort of thing was a mighty prop to lean on.

Only, Ben Spawn wasn't here, now. And Two Link wouldn't move and couldn't move without him. . . .

Syl Overdeck went back into the ranch house, got out a bottle and glass and poured himself a stiff drink. The way uncertainty and indecision were nagging him, he needed that drink.

Far over on the northern edge of the central Deer Creek Meadow, Riley Haslam was having his look at the starlight's magic on Hatchet Rim, and again the thought came to him that here indeed was as rugged and harsh a range as any man could know of. Yet, like now, it had its moments when it placed the lure of a savage beauty on a man.

Down there below, the meadow was a pool of soft star glow, and over there beyond the creek a pinpoint of yellow candlelight marked the location of the cabin. Further on across, at the meadow's southern edge, Frank Didion was also watching and waiting this thing out.

In figuring things, Haslam and Didion had been starkly realistic, weighing every circumstance as carefully as they could. They knew the worst possible move they could make was to fort up in the cabin and try and hold it. That was asking to be trapped and probably shot to ribbons behind walls that would not begin to stop the tearing progress of a rifle bullet.

Against odds, their only chance was to

stay out in the open, where they could move and shift and use the night to cover them. And so they had worked things out. As soon as the first deep dark of night hid their moves, they shifted their horses up the creek from the cabin and tied them in a heavy clump of willows.

After that they had done some careful calculation with a stub of candle, the upturned lid of a five-pound lard pail, and a cup of water. They had set the pail lid in the center of the cabin table, top side down. With some of its own hot wax, they stuck the candle stub in the middle of the lid and then filled the lid with water. And with the night settling fully in, they lighted the candle before slipping away into the wide outer dark.

Now, in the empty cabin, the candle was burning. To any one scouting the place, the gleam of candlelight would suggest occupancy of the cabin. And when, a little later, the burning candle shortened to where the water would seep in and kill the flame, it must look to that same observer as though weary men had doused the light and turned to their blankets for the night. That was the bait, the lure — that flicker of candlelight, calculated to draw any raiders in close to the cabin and so put them between the waiting guns of Riley Haslam and Frank Didion.

For this would be gun business, and dirty. How could it be anything else? It was a piece from the same pattern they'd known so well in other years. Men wanting more than they had, and determined to get it by any means and at any price. A thing like that always ended up dirty.

A man's thoughts, Haslam found, ran far and touched many things during a wait like this. Where, he mused uneasily, had so many of the good years gone? A man, to make the years count, had to have some sort of program in life. It was during the casual, careless drifting in the search of excitement and of the strong wine of adventure that a man let go of time he'd never get his hands on again. This he, Riley Haslam, had done.

He shook himself, vaguely angry. Hell! He was thinking wrong. Sure, he'd wasted a few years, riding and fighting the reckless- ness out of himself. But a man wasn't old at thirty. He had, in fact, just begun to live. And maybe that destiny business he'd been thinking about, and that he'd spoken to Janet Wilkerson about, had more to it than a man was likely to figure. Maybe it had been his destiny to serve at a hard-riding, hard- fighting, reckless trade just to prepare him for a time like this when there were things to be fought for that could count so much in all his future years.

How the starlight and the deep stillness of the night could draw the maybes out of a man . . . !

Abruptly it came to him that the pinpoint of light in the cabin was gone. The candle was out. Had anyone else besides himself and Frank Didion been watching that light? Before too long he should find out. Twenty minutes — half an hour. Long enough to judge that unwary men had fallen asleep.

A new thought hit. Maybe Cory Biggs had had it all wrong. He was a dying man when he'd told Walt Heighly about the intended raid. Biggs could have meant well, but his fading senses might have tricked him. Maybe —

Haslam shook himself again. Here was another of those damn maybes. . . .

It was instinct as much as anything else that warned him of movement off to his right. He stood high and straight, looking and listening, every sense in him keened and reaching. Now it was more than instinct. Now it was sound, the muted mutter of hoofs moving at a walk, the thin creak of saddle gear, the metallic note of a saddle mount mouthing a bit ring. The subdued murmur of a man's voice, carefully used. Then all this was stilled and faded out as the group angled below and past him and out into the meadow.

Haslam waited a little, making sure there were no stragglers still to come up, before dropping down the slope and out across the meadow himself. In him the old, cold fires were beginning to burn. If for nothing else, this was the sort of thing the past years had prepared him to handle.

It was a slow jaunt, that drift across the meadow, for a man had to move with every care and caution, with his senses ever searching and probing. Haslam knew a gust of relief when the dark shroud of the creek growth loomed ahead, and he felt his way gingerly into it. Here the presence of the night riders was strong to him.

They had crossed the creek a little distance below where he now crouched, and a slow-stirring night wind, sifting up the creek, brought him the acid reek of warm horseflesh. Also, the deep tones of a man's low-pitched but commanding voice. And right after that the night's pulsing stillness was torn wide open.

It started with a single gun letting off three evenly spaced shots, as though signaling. Then came a slashing ripple of shots and the pound of hoofs, racing in on the cabin. A rider, carried away by the avid tension of things, let go with a long, yammering yell, which several others caught up and carried along.

Haslam hit the creek, felt the waters of a shallows foam about his boots. Then he was across and driving to the outer edge of the willows on the far side. And when he broke here out into the open, he became aware of several things at once.

For one thing, the tempo of gunfire had jumped out of all proportion to what he'd figured it would be like. It was whipping in from beyond the cabin and from the open spaces of the meadow, below and to his right. But, most startling of all, either by accident or design, the lead from these guns apparently was striking at the attackers rather than the cabin, for now men were yelling again, and the yells held consternation and dismay, rather than a swift, anticipated triumph.

A couple of the shouts were reasonably coherent. One was hard and heavy with quick flaring rage, and it was the voice of Hugh Racklyn. "Watch yourself, Overdeck! You're shooting into us. Watch yourself—"

Close on the heels of this came the other shout. "Cabin's empty, Hugh! Nobody in here. This thing ain't right. We've rode into somethin' —"

"Double-cross!" yelled another, "I had a hunch —"

The shout broke off with a choking abruptness that held a deadly significance.

Riley Haslam waited to hear no more. For while he was unable to understand this defensive shooting where he'd expected only that of Frank Didion and himself, it was obvious that Racklyn and his crowd were really the confused and desperate ones.

He had held Rocking R pretty well located by their shouts, by their shooting. He dropped on one knee and shot his rifle empty, levering each try carefully and holding low against the deceptive starlight. This got almost immediate reaction in another shout of alarm.

"Now they're behind us! Let's get out of here —"

Still down on his knee, Haslam plugged fresh cartridges through the loading gate of his rifle and tried again to measure the night and all that it held. Those who had ridden to the attack were scattering now, doing a lot of blind shooting. Haslam heard bullets rip through the willows behind him, but they were high and harmless where he was concerned.

Up the meadow, toward the east, was the one side that lay open to retreat. Rocking R, pressured from the other three sides, gave back this way and, finding it clear, broke and rode for it, flinging a final half dozen wild shots.

And now, except for some riderless horses, milling and snorting here and there, night's stillness came in once more. Haslam, getting to his feet and moving cautiously over toward the cabin, let this stillness ride until it was broken by a deep and rolling shout.

"Haslam — Riley Haslam! If you're all right, give us an answer!"

Haslam gave it, at the same time knowing stark amazement. For he was answering Dr. Jason Jay.

"All right, Doc — all right! Looks like they've cleared out. Come on in!"

Now, off to Haslam's right — from where more of that unexpected shooting support had come — came another voice. This time it was Walt Heighly's.

"If it's all right with you, friend — we'll come in, too."

"I will be damned!" murmured Haslam. Then in a gladdening shout, "Welcome, everybody!"

They gathered there at the cabin, and

Haslam murmured again and again in his amazement at who had ridden this night to back his hand. Rufe Wilkerson, Walt Heighly and Mitch Connerly of Running W. From town, Doc Jay, Cash Fletcher, Pete Loftus and Sam Basile. And hovering quietly at the edge of things, Bud Caddell.

Doc explained tersely. "The kid hit town all het up, throwing things right in our face. Were we going to ride and back your hand, or weren't we? Whether we did or not, he was going to be here. And if we didn't ride, then what he thought of us wasn't fit to be told."

"Almost the same with me," put in Rufe Wilkerson gruffly. "Walt and Mitch put it on the line. They were riding tonight, and was I or wasn't I coming along? You got a way about you, Haslam. When people are for you — they're sure for you."

To cover up the gust of feeling in him, Haslam said, "There were some horses without riders milling between here and the creek. We better take a look around." And then, abruptly aware of certain incompleteness, he added anxiously, "Frank Didion should be here. He took station over south. Bud, you came in that way. You run across Frank?"

"That must have been him I heard

shooting from out there," answered Bud. "He was about where Doc and me and the others came in. Which reminds me of somethin' else. Where was Two Link in this deal? Or didn't they show?"

"Not from the way Rocking R was yelling," Haslam said. The bite of worry was in him. He moved a little apart, cupped his hands around his mouth, sent a pealing call. "Frank — Frank Didion! Answer up!"

There was no answer. Haslam moved out into the night, his voice going harshly sharp.

"Scatter and look for him. There's a good man out here — a hell of a good man —"

It was Bud Caddell who found him, and the kid's voice was thin and shaken as he called the others to him. Frank Didion lay full length on top of his rifle, his head resting on one forearm. Just like a man sleeping. Only, this was a sleep from which there was no rousing. Frank Didion had been shot through the heart. A wild, chance bullet from one of those stampeded Rocking R guns. . . .

Doc Jay's face was hard-graven in the flickering light of the match which he held while he made swift examination. And his voice was a softened rumble as he spoke words he'd used before.

"Somewhere they die. . . ."

It did no good to find three riderless

horses bearing the Rocking R iron, nor to discover that the men who had ridden these animals were down and everlastingly still in the area between the cabin and the creek. The fact that one of these riders was old Albie Tharp meant nothing except that Doc Jay's words could apply to enemy as well as friend. Nor did it do any good to realize that a second of these riders was Pres Hoag, the Rocking R foreman.

Only if Hugh Racklyn lay dead out there would it have helped at all, thought Riley Haslam, darkly empty. And it was doubtful that would have helped, either. For Frank Didion was gone, and there was no leavening substitute.

Left only with the certainty that he must locate Hugh Racklyn and come up with him and face him and finish it, one way or the other, for good and all. Maybe he should have thought of Syl Overdeck, too. But somehow Overdeck didn't seem to count. Not like Hugh Racklyn did.

Out at Two Link headquarters, Syl Overdeck was still waiting for the return of Ben Spawn. By this time, Overdeck had convinced himself that Spawn had been scouting either Rocking R or Spoon headquarters, or both, and found something to support his argument that Hugh Racklyn had never meant to go through with the raid, but had intended a double-cross from the first.

It was indicative of the character of Syl Overdeck that he should think thus. It was his great weakness, this tendency to believe what he wanted to believe in the face of crisis or extreme difficulty. Yeah, he told himself, Ben Spawn would be along any time now. . . .

Through the open window at his side, Overdeck picked up the first faint clump of approaching hoofs. He listened, head slightly tipped. One horse. This would be Spawn. Restless, half relieved, half angry, Overdeck stepped out on the ranch house porch. Through the starlight he picked up rider and horse and they came straight to him. Overdeck threw his thin and nasally complaining question.

"God damn it, Ben — where you been?"

The answer wasn't in Ben Spawn's voice at all. And the words dropped an icy pressure all through Overdeck.

"Bum guess, Overdeck! Now I'm asking — where were you? I had Rocking R at Deer Creek for that raid, but Two Link didn't show. If you were there, Overdeck, you did no fighting. Believe I warned you not to double-cross me. You were to hit from the south when I hit from the north. You were to wait for that first three-shot signal and then charge in. Remember, Overdeck? That's what you promised to do. But you didn't do it. You double-crossed me, and I warned you not to —"

Overdeck frantically found voice and movement, grabbing for his gun as he cried out.

"Wait, Hugh — wait! I'd have been there, only —"

"No onlys," droned Hugh Racklyn, shooting across his saddle. He'd had a naked gun in his fist when he rode into Two Link, and now he threw that blasting slug into the lank figure standing against the light of the open door.

Syl Overdeck reeled, then jackknifed forward and started down. Hugh Racklyn drove another slug into him as he fell.

Sounded a muffled yell in the Two Link bunkhouse and a man appeared in the door of the building, only to duck wildly back as Racklyn slammed a bullet into the wall close alongside. Then Racklyn spun his horse and rode away.

"That," he told himself, "is something I should have done long ago. Now for Haslam. After that, we'll see!"

# CHAPTER XIII

It was pushing midnight by the time they reached town with Frank Didion's body. Riley Haslam had had little to say. Briefly and bleakly he'd thanked those who had ridden to help him in this thing. Then he'd taken the lead rope of Frank Didion's horse, with its silent, sagging burden, and headed for town, deep sunk in a locked-out silence.

His thoughts went round and round in a bitter circle, dull and stunned on most things, yet savagely clear on the fact that Frank Didion was dead, and that he'd died for that ancient, empty cause of another man's interests. Dying just as surely for Spoon interests as he might have for Two Link, and to no better purpose.

Haslam remembered how he and Didion had talked that day when they reached town after defying and quitting Two Link. Of the thought they'd had of riding across the mountains together. Had they done that, then Frank would have been alive this moment. But they hadn't made the ride.

The proposition to take over Spoon had been offered and accepted, and so now Frank was dead.

He hardly remembered crossing the river at the ford, and he was startled when a few late lights of town were suddenly in front of him. And then, just as suddenly, it seemed he didn't know where to go or what to do.

It was Doc Jay who solved this problem for him, good old Doc Jay and Cash Fletcher and young Bud Caddell. Doc pulled the lead rope from his hand and Doc's big voice was a quiet rumble.

"From here on this is my chore, Riley. Bud here and I will take care of things. You go along with Cash and get some rest. Don't make me argue with you, man. You know I'm right."

Still for a moment, Haslam nodded as he slid from his saddle. "All right, Doc. Thanks."

He followed Cash Fletcher into the Staghorn and past the bar and up the stairs to Fletcher's room. In there, when Fletcher got the light going, he sat on the edge of the spare bunk, shoulders low-hunched, hands sagging loose between his knees. Cash Fletcher handed him a water glass holding a heavy four fingers of whiskey and he downed the liquor in two gulps. Fletcher, wielding a deft bottle, had the glass refilled to the same measure before Haslam could put it aside. So he drank this, too, and then obeyed automatically when Fletcher said:

"Stretch out and take it easy."

It was good to lie there, not even trying for conscious thought, while the whiskey loosened him up and softened that knotted inside tension. And the jolting impact of it was a mounting wave of warm drowsiness that pushed everything else back into a distant and hazy blur.

Five minutes later he was asleep. Cash Fletcher covered him with a blanket, put out the light and left the room.

When Haslam awoke the next morning, Cash Fletcher had just finished shaving. Haslam pushed aside the blanket, sat up. His tongue felt thick, his head heavy. He borrowed Fletcher's razor, then had a good wash, emptying the last of the water in the big white pitcher over his head. When he'd toweled himself dry he was ready to face the day with less distaste. Not until they were ready to leave the room did Cash Fletcher make any direct remarks. But now he spoke.

"Here is something you should know about, Riley. Last night after you went to sleep, I went back downstairs. Pretty soon Doc Jay and Bud Caddell came in. Under the circumstances I felt we could all do with a drink, so I poured one at the bar. About that time a pair of Two Link riders came in. They weren't looking for any trouble. Far from it. They were pulling out, leaving this range for good, and they wanted a bottle to keep them company on the ride across the mountains. They had some interesting news to leave behind. Syl Overdeck is dead."

Riley Haslam jerked around. "Overdeck — dead! How —"

"Hugh Racklyn killed him. Rode in at Two Link last night and shot Overdeck while he stood on the porch of his own ranch house. After that, Racklyn threw a shot at the bunkhouse and then rode out. The hands in the Two Link bunkhouse heard Overdeck yell, just before the shots. They heard him yell, 'Wait, Hugh — wait!' so they knew it was Racklyn who did it."

"But they were supposed to have sided together to get me," Haslam blurted.

Cash Fletcher nodded quickly. "That's just it. According to the story by Cory Biggs, they were going to raid you together. Well, we know that Racklyn and his Rocking R crowd were there last night, but was there any sign of Overdeck and his Two Link? None at all that I know of. Maybe Overdeck figured things that way, for he's ever been

303

the sly and foxy one. I wouldn't be surprised if he hadn't figured some kind of a double-cross on Racklyn. And Racklyn, after taking a pretty rough going over, looked up Overdeck and called him. That's the way it looks to me."

Haslam nodded grimly. "Whatever the reason, with Overdeck dead — that's that. And it leaves — just Racklyn!"

Again Fletcher gave that quick nod. "Just Hugh Racklyn. If it was the other way around I'd know a lot less concern. For make no mistake, friend, whatever else he may be, Hugh Racklyn is no coward. He may be two-thirds raw brute, he may be all cow thief. He may be anything else you want to name him. But never doubt his fundamental guts!"

Cash Fletcher had had early breakfast, so now Riley Haslam went into the Staghorn dining room alone. He'd hardly taken a seat at a table when Janet Wilkerson came in, vivid as a flower with the whipped-up coloring of early-morning riding. But she was gravely sober as she came quickly to his table and sat down across from him.

"Father told me all about it," she said. "About your friend, Frank Didion. You must know, Riley, how sorry I am —"

She meant it, all right, for her voice ran

out into huskiness and she dabbed at her eyes with the back of her hand. "It just seems," she added, half whispering, "that anything which hurts you, hurts me, too. It may sound a little crazy, but it's really the truth."

Looking at her, Haslam knew a great and deep gentleness. He reached across the table, captured one of her hands. "You rode into town this early to tell me that?"

She nodded. "That's part of it. The rest is — you must let it stop here, Riley. If you feel that — that because of your friend, you must go after Hugh Racklyn —"

"I feel that way," cut in Haslam. "It's the way it must be."

"But — why?" cried Janet softly. "You've destroyed Hugh Racklyn in these parts just as surely as though you'd — you'd killed him. He has no single friend left. He stands for exactly what he is in the eyes of every decent person. He can't last under those conditions. He'll just have to leave — Oh, Riley — you —"

"Not that simple," Haslam told her. "Racklyn shapes up now as a grizzly on the loose. I've the feeling that even if I wasn't after him, he'd still be after me. This is just one of those things that the fates drop right in front of you, and you can't do a thing about it but accept it."

She began a soft, little-girl whimper and a couple of tears squeezed out and rolled down her cheeks.

"Here — here!" chided Haslam gently. "That'll never do. Now let's forget about Hugh Racklyn. Just you sit there so I can look at you and know there's goodness and gentleness in the world as well as other things. You know — I don't believe I've ever said flatly that I love you. But I do — I surely do."

He saw her catch her breath, saw the tiny pulse beat in the hollow of her throat, and her eyes were soft, shining through her tears.

At the door of the dining room someone cleared his throat. It was the town marshal, Sam Basile. Catching the look on Basile's face, Haslam came to his feet, and his voice rang harshly.

"What is it, Basile?"

"Hugh Racklyn! He's got that kid rider, Caddell, cornered down at the livery. If it matters to you — you better get down there —"

"You!" charged Haslam furiously. "You're town marshal. What —"

The flush of his great shame whipped across Basile's face, then left it gray and tired and futile. "I know my limits," he said woodenly. "And I'm just not big enough for this."

Haslam shoved the man aside savagely as he went past him, and he was running when he reached the street. How far from the Staghorn to the livery? The whole length of town — clear past the street's slight turn. Would it be too far?

Haslam's ears were straining for the first sound of gunfire, but he got past the street's angle and morning's quiet still held. Now he could see the front of the livery but there was no one in sight. Maybe Basile had given it to him wrong. Maybe —

Fifty yards from the livery he slowed to a walk, the breath of exertion running in and out of him deeply. He came in toward the shadowy tunnel beyond the livery door with ever increasing caution. And finally he was at the edge of it and pausing, listening.

There was no sound within the stable, but there was a voice out past the corner and around toward the back, by the corrals. Haslam stepped past the corner.

There was a bulgy-eyed, fear-stupefied stable roustabout there, as well as Bud Caddell. They stood side by side, their backs to the corral fence. Bud had a hayfork in his hands, but carried no other weapon.

Some ten paces away from them was Hugh Racklyn, standing with feet a trifle spread and big shoulders pitched forward, and his words were lashing at Bud Caddell.

"I'm not going to ask you again, Caddell. Where's Haslam? He in town, or out on Deer Creek?"

Bud's face was white, his lips pinched thin. But his jaw was stubborn and his glance fixed and level. His answer came low, but clear, as he lied gallantly.

"I tell you I don't know where he is, Racklyn. He fired me yesterday noon. I don't know where he is."

There was a strange and wild shagginess about Hugh Racklyn, so it seemed to Haslam. And in this tight-drawn moment, it was strange indeed that he should remember what Cash Fletcher had said about Racklyn.

"He may be two-thirds raw brute —"

"Right here, Racklyn," said Haslam, "if it's me you're looking for!"

Hugh Racklyn came around, ponderous as a grizzly, yet just as swiftly. And Riley Haslam thought again that here was a man who had let go of a vital something that marked the difference between upright dignity and shambling retrogression. Even the sound that erupted from Racklyn's lips was more inarticulate growl than meaningful words. And with the sound, Hugh Racklyn went for it.

Riley Haslam, waiting and watching for that breaking move, took a long stride to the left which dropped into a half-crouch, drawing as he went, and shooting even as his gun tipped level and free from the holster. It was a coordinated move which a United States deputy marshal had once taught him, long ago. Now he did not consciously plan it and use it. It just came instinctively.

The theory was, so the deputy marshal had explained, that a gunfighter, fixed to draw and throw a shot at a set target, would, once he'd started his move, almost surely drive the slug into that area, even though the target had slipped out of it. He would correct for his second shot, of course, but he would have wasted that vital first shot.

So it was now. Racklyn had been very fast with his draw, and Riley Haslam sensed that Racklyn had actually beaten him to that first shot. Yet he felt no impact blow, knew Racklyn had missed. And he hadn't!

He saw Racklyn stagger, waver, and go fatally slow in trying to get off his second shot. And Haslam got there ahead this time, and followed with a third thudding blast.

Hugh Racklyn dropped his gun, coughed in a deep, shuddering way, then melted down in sprawled stillness.

Over against the corral fence the terrified stable roustabout dropped into a sitting position, lowered his head against his knees and blubbered his relief.

Bud Caddell dropped his hayfork and came over to Riley Haslam.

"— not hit, boss — you're not hit —"

Haslam shook his head, so Bud went on, as though finding relief in words.

"I came down to look after our broncs, and while I was workin' them, here of a sudden Racklyn was. He began asking questions, getting rougher and rougher —"

Haslam dropped a hand on Bud's arm. "But you didn't tell him, did you, kid? Frank — Frank Didion would have been damned proud of you this morning."

He knew what that rolling gun thunder would do. It would bring them from every angle and corner with their questions. He turned away.

"You tell them about it, Bud."

But the first one to reach him when he stepped into the clear of the street again, was no one Bud Caddell could have said anything to.

It was Janet Wilkerson, running like a

little girl before the wind, and her relief was a wrenched sobbing as she caught at him and clung to him.

He saw no one else, heard no one else. Here was an ending and here was a beginning.

Doc Jay, seeing and understanding, said, "And somewhere they live!"

We hope you have enjoyed this Large Print book. Other Thorndike Press or Chivers Press Large Print books are available at your library or directly from the publishers.

For more information about current and upcoming titles, please call or write, without obligation, to:

Thorndike Press
P.O. Box 159
Thorndike, Maine 04986 USA
Tel. (800) 223-1244 or (800) 223-6121

OR

Chivers Press Limited
Windsor Bridge Road
Bath BA2 3AX
England
Tel. (0225) 335336

All our Large Print titles are designed for easy reading, and all our books are made to last.